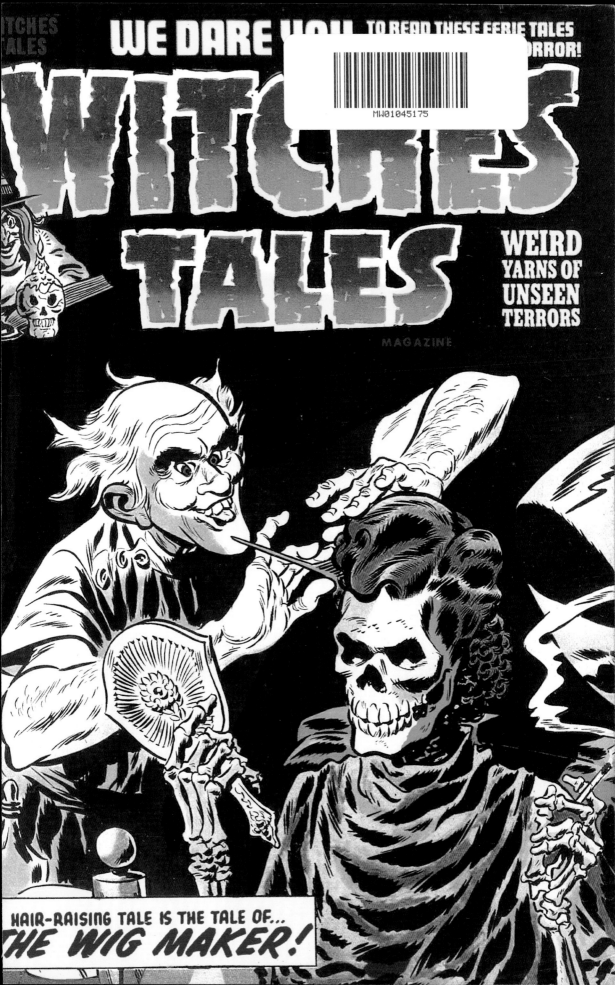

Draw This Car

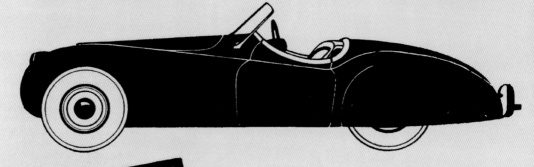

WITCHES TALES, FEBRUARY, 1953, VOL. 1, NO. 23, IS PUBLISHED BI-MONTHLY by WITCHES TALES, INC., 1860 Broadway, New York 23, N. Y. Entered as second class matter at the Post Office at New York, N. Y., under the Act of March, 3, 1879. Single copies, 10c. Subscription rates, 10 issues for $1.00 in the U. S. and possessions, elsewhere $1.50. All names in this periodical are entirely fictitious and no identification with actual persons is intended. Contents copyrighted, 1953, by Witches Tales, Inc., New York, City. Printed in the U.S.A. Title registered in U. S. Patent Office.

Dear Readers

You wanted it! Now, you've got it -- a recipe of horror in two parts shock and one part fancy. This latest WITCHES TALES is really something to chill your spine -- and tickle your funny bone!

At first, these stories put a smile on your face -- and then fear in your heart. They butter you up with a feather, only to hammer you with terror! Chuckle in the night with them -- and scream in the shadows!

Let's hear your reaction to this fanciful, frightful brew of seering suspense and terrorific tales with that touch of the bizarre! Your opinions as expressed in your letters are what we want, so write as you think ... and don't spare the horses!

And here's something else. There is a surprise coming to you in next month's issue of WITCHES TALES.

It's, once again, that extra something you've gotten in the past. But, all that can be said now is that it's a blue-ribbon package of terror all prepared for you. So watch for it ... watch out for shock!

So, from here to hysteria, it's WITCHES TALES ... and don't forget to write! The address of this prince of shock is....

WITCHES TALES
1860 Broadway
New York 23, N. Y.

WITCHES TALES Contents NO. 23

FOR THE MOST PART, THIS WAS THE STORY OF HENRY SMALL'S LIFE... RUNNING FROM THE POLICE! HENRY WAS A HUCKSTER...A PEDDLER...A CON-MAN! HIS PRIME ASSET WAS TALK--BACKED UP WITH A PAIR OF FAST FEET...AND HE PUT THE LATTER TO USE AS HE RAN INTO A TRAIN DEPOT!

A SATISFACTORY PLACE!...NOISE... CROWDS...PEOPLE...

PEOPLE! ZOWIE! LOOK WHAT'S THERE!

THERE, NOT MORE THAN FIFTY PACES FROM HENRY SMALL, WAS A MAN. TEN-GALLON HAT, HIGH-BUTTON SHOES, STARCHED COLLAR, PEARL-STUDDED VEST...A RURAL SORE-THUMB IN AN URBAN TRAIN STATION!

WELCOME TO THE BIG CITY

TOKENS 15¢

NO COPS... ...AROUND!

HENRY SIDLED UP TO THE MAN, WAITED A FEW SECONDS, AND THEN BEGAN.

MISTUH...PSS-T! DON'T SAY A WORD, NOT A SOLITARY SYLLABLE. I NEED HELP. YOU'VE GOT TO HELP ME, YOU SEE--SOMEBODY STOLE MY WALLET. I'M STUCK... WITHOUT A PENNY. PLEASE...HELP ME!

SUH, I DON'T KNOW..

LOOK! LOOK AT THIS RING. IT--IT'S AN HEIRLOOM. MY POOR SICK MOTHER BEQUEATHED IT TO ME ON HER DEATH BED. THIS SOLID RUBY IS ALL I HAVE LEFT TO MY NAME. WOULD YOU LIKE TO BUY IT?

HOPE TO DIE, IF IT'S NOT REAL! WOULD MY POOR SICK MOTHER GIVE ME A FAKE? NOT MY POOR SICK MOTHER! ...FOR FIFTY DOLLARS.

WELL, NOW...A MAN FROM BOONE COUNTY NEVER LEAVES A FELLOW HUMAN-BEIN' IN THE LURCH, NO SIR! SUH...I WILL BUY YOUR RING!

A DEAL CONSUMMATED! YOU WILL NEVER REGRET IT. YOU HAVE A HEART OF GOLD...SOMETHING THIS WORLD NEEDS MORE OF! THANK YOU, OH, THANK YOU!

SAY NUTHIN' MORE, CHILD! GLAD TO HELP OUT...RIGHT GLAD!

HENRY SMALL EXCHANGED THE RING FOR THE STRANGER'S FIFTY DOLLARS. IT WAS AN HONORABLE TRANSACTION ON A SMALL SCALE, OF COURSE...

2

SECONDS PASSED BEFORE...

IT'S... GLASS!

THE SHOUT COULD BE HEARD THROUGH THE TERMINAL'S MARBLE HALLS! ITS VIBRATIONS ENTERED SMALL'S EARS, RAN THROUGH HIS BODY, ACTIVATED HIS LEGS, PROPELLED HIS FEET. SO... SMALL RAN...

AH'VE... BEEN... TRICKED!

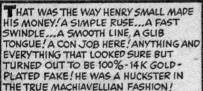

THAT WAS THE WAY HENRY SMALL MADE HIS MONEY! A SIMPLE RUSE... A FAST SWINDLE... A SMOOTH LINE, A GLIB TONGUE! A CON JOB HERE! ANYTHING AND EVERYTHING THAT LOOKED SURE BUT TURNED OUT TO BE 100% - 14K GOLD-PLATED FAKE! HE WAS A HUCKSTER IN THE TRUE MACHIAVELLIAN FASHION!

PSS-T! HEY, BUDDIE... WOULD YOU LIKE TO PURCHASE A CIGARETTE CASE? SOLID GOLD... SHINES LIKE A MIRROR... HOLDS TWENTY CIGARETTES! LIGHTS UP EVERYTIME YOU USE IT! I GOT TO GET RID OF IT... VERY FAST! IT'S YOURS... FOR CHEAP... CHEAP... CHEAP!

IF YOU ARE TALKING TO ME, WISEACRE ... PLEASE UN-HAND DA GARMENT! THEN... WE WILL EXCHANGE GAB!

(GULP!) SURE--SURE THING! I LOST MY HEAD! I... UH... WOULD LIKE TO RID MYSELF OF THIS CASE! A BARGAIN IS NOT THE WORD FOR THIS TRANSACTION. IT'S A... STEAL... A REAL STEAL!

DA THING LOOKS GOOD T'ME! IT IS IMPRESSING ME! I SHALL PAY YOU A DOUBLE-SAW FOR IT,... AND NOT A PLUG NICKEL MORE! DIS IS MY LAST WORD!

TWENTY BUCKS! FOR THIS! I... UH... MEAN-- FOR THIS? WELL, I DON'T KNOW! OKAY! SOLD!

HERE IS DA LOOT! NOW, MY GOOD MAN ... I WOULD APPRECIATE IT IF YOU WILL BE OFF! COP... A... WALK!

SMALL DID AS HIS CUSTOMER BECKONED. HE LEFT IN A SLOW WALK.... IN A MORE-THAN-ADEQUATE TROT... THEN IN A VERY FAST RUN! SECONDS LATER...

...DA GUY IS A CROOK!

CLICK

3

AGAIN, HENRY SMALL'S FAST TALK HAD NETTED HIM A GAIN, BUT THIS TIME IT WAS NOT TO GO UNDISTURBED. HIS LATEST VICTIM DID NOT STEP OFF THE TRAIN. HE WAS NOT BORN YESTERDAY. HE HAD BEEN AROUND... AROUND A LOT OF VERY "INFLUENTIAL" PEOPLE...

IN THE PAST I AM DOING SOMETHING FOR YOU! NOW... RECIPROCATE! I WANT FOR YOU T'DIG UP DIS MOUSEY CHARACTER.... DAT I AM TELLING YOU ABOUT,... AND KINDLY PUT DA SCREWS ON HIM. I WOULD GREATLY APPRECIATE IT...IF YOU WOULD RUB HIM OUT!

TO ME...DIS CHARACTER SOUNDS LIKE...HENRY SMALL.

I AGREE!

SO...THE HUNT FOR HENRY SMALL BEGAN!

THE WORD SPREAD! HENRY SMALL...THE HUCKSTER... WAS ON DEATH'S AGENDA! THE DRAGNET CLOSED IN... UNTIL...

HENRY! COME QUIETLY...OR I'LL BLOW YOUR BRAINS OUT!

I AGREE!

HENRY, THE MARK HAS BEEN PUT ON YOU! DIS IS A NICE PLACE TO PUT YOU AWAY... QUIET, OUT OF DA WAY, ETC. YOU WILL ROT HERE, HENRY!

I AGREE!

B-BUT YOU CAN'T DO THIS. WHAT'VE I DONE TO YOU BOYS? I HAVEN'T PUT ANYTHING OVER ON YOU! I'M CLEAN, LET ME GO, BOYS! LET...ME...GO!

I COULD MAKE YOU RICH, BOYS! RICH! RICH! RICH! I GOT SOME GOLD-MINING STOCK! IT--IT'S YOURS. TAKE IT OFF MY HANDS! ONLY... LET ME GO!

NO CAN DO!

GOLD?!

I DON'T AGREE, ALPHA! HENRY'S GOT GOLD. WE GOT NOTHIN'! WE COULD BE RICH! ALL WE GOTTA DO IS....LET HENRY GO! WHA'D'YA SAY, ALPHA? COME ON! HUH, ALPHA?

WELL, NOW ....I DON'T KNOW...

YOU'LL BE RICH! RICH... RICH...

4

THE END

5

MISTER MASTER

Larry Benson was taking his usual after-dinner walk. He was walking casually ... slowly ...

And then suddenly he saw this ghome-like figure walking towards him. "He sure is a funny one," he said to himself.

"Hello, Mr. Benson," the little man said to Larry.

"Huh?" Larry sounded. "Hello, sir, but how did you know my name? I don't think I know *you*."

"No, Mr. Benson, you don't know me, but I know you very well. I've been watching you closely for quite a while ..."

"Watching me closely? What do you mean by that?" This all seemed so stupid and silly to Larry. "Why are you so interested in me, Mr. . . . . ."

"Mr. Master is my name, sir. Well, you see I was a very good friend of your father's, and when he died I promised I'd look after you ..."

"But, my father died in an asylum! Were you a doctor there?" Larry stared at the little man and wondered how his father could ever become friendly with a strange creature like that.

"No," the little man laughed. "No, I wasn't a doctor. But I *was* very close to him."

Suddenly there was a voice ... "Hey, Larry, how have you been?" It was Joe Stewart, Larry's neighbor.

"Oh, hello, Joe. I'd like you to meet Mr. Master, a friend of my father's!"

"Huh?" said Joe Stewart. "What are you talking about?"

"I said I'd like you to meet Mr. Master!" Larry was reasonably annoyed.

"Who's Mr. Master?" Joe didn't know what hit him.

Mr. Master was a friend of my father's..."

"I heard that, but where is he?"

"Now stop being funny, Joe! I'm sorry about all this, Mr. Master." Larry turned to his little friend with a beg-pardon look on his face.

"It's all right, Larry," said Mr. Master. "That's the way your father's friends treated me!"

"I'm getting out of here," shouted Joe Stewart. And he did!

Minutes later, Larry Benson presented Mr. Master to his wife, Martha.

"But, Larry, what are you talking about? There's no man with you!"

"Martha! Stop talking like that! I don't think you're being fair to Mr. Master!"

"Don't get excited," interrupted Mr. Master, "they always talk like that about me!"

"But, why, Mr. Master? I don't understand all this! Do you think it's fair?"

"It's not for us to judge, Larry. If they don't want to accept me, then there's noth- we can do about it!" The little man just shook his head.

"Don't worry, Mr. Master, they're going to accept you — or else!"

Days later, the "or else" took place ...

"Gee, thanks for sticking up for me, Larry! You're just like your father was!"

"That's all right, Mr. Master. You'd probably do the same for me. At least everyone *here* accepts you! Hey, Napoleon, come here and talk with us!"

Mother Mongoose's NURSERY CRIMES

"As I was going along, long, long...

Singing a comical song, song, song!

They all thought my singing was wrong, wrong, wrong.

BOINNNNNG!

Then all I heard was bong, bong, bong!"

Mother Mongoose's NURSERY CRIMES

"Solomon Grundy saw her on a Monday

Joy supreme it was his fun day!

Change of plans. It was his run day!

Boy, oh boy! Did he wish it was Sunday!"

SIR IVAN GWAINE HAS WON *AGAIN!* OUR FEARLESS KNIGHT HAS *MASTERED* THE *KING'S TOURNAMENT!*

I HAVE FARED WELL, AS HEAVEN ORDAINED, BUT FORSOOTH--'TIS MUCH TOO VALIANT A KNIGHT I HAVE FACED NOT TO GO UNHERALDED! RISE SIR GERALD--THOU HAST BEEN A *WORTHY* OPPONENT!

I PAY HOMAGE TO YOUR *SKILL*, SIR IVAN! YOU HAVE MY PLEDGE OF ALLEGIANCE IN ANY UNDERTAKING THOU MAY TAKE!

MY *DEAREST* IVAN! HOW MY HEART *FLUTTERED* WHEN I SAW THEE BEFORE ME! YOU ARE THE BRAVEST KNIGHT OF THEM ALL!

ELIZABETH--IT IS FOR *THEE* THAT I RODE AND FOUGHT! LET ALL WHO WITNESSED THIS MEET KNOW THAT I, SIR IVAN GWAINE OF HAMPSHIRE-- HAVE GIVEN THEE MY *HEART!*

DO THEY NOT MAKE A CHARMING COUPLE, SIR HUGO? SIR GWAINE HAS INDEED DISTINGUISHED HIMSELF AS MOST CAPABLY AS THOU!

NOT SO, FITZHUGH! KNOW THEE THAT *I* AM THE KING'S *EXECUTIONER*--AND AS SUCH--I AM *THE BEST KNIGHT* OF ALL! MY BATTLE SCARS, MY *UGLINESS* ARE PROOF OF MY *SUPREMACY!*

KING JOHN OF BRITAIN HAD INDEED MANY VALIANT KNIGHTS--BUT NONE SO POPULAR AS SIR IVAN GWAINE. INDEED-- ALL KNEW THAT HE AND ELIZABETH, THE KING'S DAUGHTER, HAD ANNOUNCED THEIR BETROTHAL, THUS--AT THE CASTLE AFTERWARDS...

RISE MY BROTHER KNIGHTS AND VASSALS! A TOAST TO *ELIZABETH*, MY DAUGHTER-- AND HER FEARLESS GENTLEMAN-- A TOAST TO *SIR GWAINE!*

HEAR! HEAR!

TO THE *BEST* KNIGHT OF THEM ALL!

HOLD! I, HUGO LAVON OF BLACKMORE-- THE KING'S EXECUTIONER...THE BLACK KNIGHT...SAY HOLD!

I HAVE TOO LONG LISTENED TO THE SLANDERS WHISPERED ABOUT ME BY KNIGHTS WHO THINK THIS BOY WITH THE GOLDEN HAIR--THIS BEARDLESS PUPPY WITH HIS MAIDEN'S FACE--IS MORE SKILLED THAN I! I MUST SPEAK! I BEG OF THEE PROPER ACKNOWLEDGEMENT, SIRE!

YAY, I AM THE UGLIEST MAN IN THE KINGDOM... MY BLOODY SCARS MAKE ME SO! BUT IT IS THIS UGLINESS WHICH HAS MADE ME THY EXECUTIONER, AND BEARS WITNESS TO MY MASTERY!

CALM THYSELF, SIR HUGO! WE HAVE MEANT THEE NO SHAME. INDEED--THERE IS NO ONE IN MY ENTIRE REALM TO MATCH THY ARMS AND CUNNING! MY DAUGHTER APOLOGIZES FOR HER RASH WORDS!

NAY! I WILL NOT HAVE AN UGLY MONSTER BULLY US INTO COWED SUBMISSION! SIR GWAINE HAS PROVEN HIMSELF TODAY--AND NO ONE CAN DENY IT! NOT EVEN THEE, BLACK KNIGHT!

I AM HUMBLED...FOR I WILL NOT DEFY MY PROTECTOR, THY FATHER BUT... WERE THEE A KNIGHT WHO SPOKE THOSE VAINGLORIOUS WORDS, I WOULD SPEW THEE IN TWO UPON MY SWORD!

THEN HAVE AT IT, MY JEALOUS COCK! I CANNOT LET YOUR INSULT TO MY FAIR LADY GO UNANSWERED.

SIR GWAINE! STOP!

TOO LATE, MY LORD! I CHALLENGE THY EXECUTIONER TO A TRIAL BY MORTAL COMBAT!

SO BE IT! SIR HUGO-- SINCE YOU ARE THE CHALLENGED PARTY, YOU HAVE THE CHOICE OF WEAPONS!

MY CHOICE IS--THE COMPLETE COMBAT ARMS OF THE BATTLE KNIGHT! AGREED!

3

THAT NEXT MORNING -- THE TRIAL BY COMBAT BEGAN!

CRASHH!

CLANG!

CRACK!

CRAASHH!

K'LONG!

KRANGGG!

ON AND ON THEY FOUGHT~RIPPING, TEARING, CUTTING MAIMING ONE ANOTHER, UNTIL~

THIS IS YOUR ~~~ FINISH ~~~ SIR GWAINS ~~~ YOUR *FINISH* ~~

NO! NO! AGGHHH!

SIR GWAINE IS THE VICTOR! ALL HAIL THE VICTOR!

YOU HAVE DONE ADMIRABLY, SIR GWAINE! AND YOU SHALL HAVE YOUR REWARD~~! THE *HIGHEST* REWARD OF THIS LAND! ALL MY NOBLES AND LADIES SHALL FOREVER ACKNOWLEDGE YOUR VICTORY OVER SIR HUGO!

AND TWO MONTHS AFTERWARDS--ON THE KING'S JOUSTING FIELDS,

HIS MAJESTY HAS BEEN MOST *GRACIOUS* TO THEE, SIR GWAINE! TRULY~ THE HONOR HE BESTOWED UPON THEE CANNOT BE EXCELLED!

IT WAS MOST KIND OF HIM, ROBERT ~BUT ONLY *LOGICAL* ~FOR I AM NOW THE *PERFECT CHOICE!* IT MATTERS NOT THAT ELIZABETH HAS BROKEN HER ENGAGEMENT TROTH TO ME! *OTHER* AFFAIRS ARE MORE URGENT!

SO SAYING, OUT STEPPED SIR IVAN GWAINE FROM HIS TENT THAT BRIGHT SUNNY DAY IN MERRY ENGLAND--CHANGED BY DAILY BATTLE AND COMBAT--TO THE *UGLIEST* MAN IN THE *KINGDOM*-- THE *GREATEST* KNIGHT OF ALL--THE KING'S EXECUTIONER--THE *BLACK KNIGHT!*

The End

5

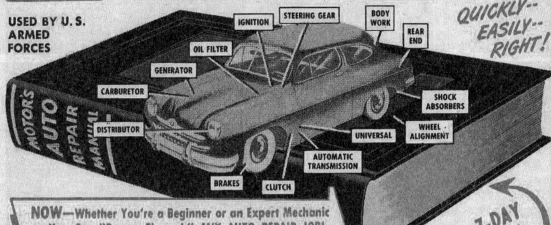

HERE IS A TALE TO MAKE YOUR HAIR STAND ON END! IT'S A REAL SHOCK SHAMPOO CALLED THE...

THE WIG-MAKER

JIMINY-HOSEPHAT! THIS SWEET LI'L OLE HAIR! SOFT 'N PURRIN' LIK' A BABY IN-FANT-ILE KITTY! I SUR' GIT GOOD STOCK...WHEN I WANTA!

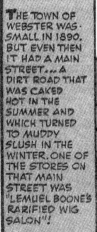

THE TOWN OF WEBSTER WAS SMALL IN 1890. BUT EVEN THEN IT HAD A MAIN STREET... A DIRT ROAD THAT WAS CAKED HOT IN THE SUMMER AND WHICH TURNED TO MUDDY SLUSH IN THE WINTER. ONE OF THE STORES ON THAT MAIN STREET WAS "LEMUEL BOONE'S RARIFIED WIG SALON"!

HOWDY DO, MR. AVERILL? NEVAH 'PECTED TA SEE YOU IN HEAH! COMES AS A RIGHT BIG SUH-PRISE TA ME! BUT... A PLEASANT ONE! YESIRREE!

I'VE BEEN HOLD-ING OFF THIS... UH...VISIT AS LONG AS POSSIBLE, LEM. YOU CAN UNDERSTAND WHY!

TING-A-LING!

YA DON'T HAVTA SAY IT TWIC'T, MR. AVERILL. I AM THE SPITTIN' IMAGE OF DEE-CORUM! 'COURSE T'AIN'T NUTHIN' TA BE ASHAMED OF...BALD-NESS, I MEAN!

NEVERTHELESS, I HAVE LOST MY HAIR! A MAN ...AHEM...IN MY POSITION...AHEM... WITH THE WOMEN CAN-NOT AFFORD SUCH A SLUR! YOU WILL MAKE ME A WIG! I STRESS EXACT DUPLICATION OF MY FORMER HAIR!

1

BLONDE, WAVY HAIR! YOU WILL TRY YOUR BEST! RIGHT?

DON'T WORRY, MR. AVERILL! YA WON'T BE ABLE TA TELL YOUR NEW MANE FUM YOUR OLD ONE! YA JES' LEAVE THET JOB TA ME!

HOW DID LEM BOONE GET THE HAIR FOR HIS WIGS? ESPECIALLY IN A REMOTE TOWN LIKE WEBSTER? LET US FOLLOW HIM...AND SEE! THAT NIGHT, HE CLOSED HIS SHOP...

THE WAY YA WEAR YA HAIR... ♪♫

...AND, HITCHING UP HIS TROUSERS, HE FOLLOWED MAIN STREET UNTIL IT CURVED CLEAR OUT OF TOWN AND DIPPED INTO THE CEMETERY! HE OPENED THE RUSTY GATE...

♪♫ THET LI'L OLE WAY YA LOOK TOO-NIGHT... ♪

...HE WALKED, AND TOOK A SHOVEL HIDDEN IN THE HOLLOW OF A TREE! INSPECTING THE GROUND, HE FINALLY FOUND WHAT HE WANTED! THEN, HE BEGAN TO DIG...

♪♫ WE MAY NEVAH NEVAH MEET AGAIN... ♫

...SCOOPING OUT THE SOFT EARTH OVER A GRAVE, TWO FEET...THREE... SIX FEET DOWN...THEN...THE HARD CLUNK OF A COFFIN! SMILING, HE CREAKED OPEN THE COFFIN'S LID...

NO...NO! YA CAIN'T TAKE THET... ♫

...HE SAW AN AGE-OLD SKELETON! HIS EYES LIT UP AS HE WITH-DREW THE HATCHET FROM HIS BELT! THIS WAS A GOOD CATCH! SO, WITH A FULL, DETERMINED SWING...

THWACK!

...AWAY FUM ME...BABY! ♪♫

...HE SEPARATED THE SKELETON FROM ITS HAIR! HE THEN CLOSED THE COFFIN'S LID, REFILLED THE GRAVE, HID THE SHOVEL, AND LEFT THE CEMETERY... WAVING A SHOCK OF BLONDE, WAVY HAIR!

2

AFTER SOME MECHANICS, LEM HAD A FINISHED WIG! AND WHEN AVERILL CAME IN...

IT'S A...*MIRACLE*, LEM! I FEEL LIKE MY OLD SELF! A *STUPENDOUS* JOB!

THANK YA, MR. AVERILL! I KNEW YA'D 'PREC-I-ATE IT! NOW... IF I CUD JES' *COLLECT* MY FEE...

THERE YOU ARE, LEM! YOU DESERVE EVERY PENNY OF IT! *YOU'LL GO PLACES!*

TWENNY...TWENNY-FIVE...SURE, MR. AVERILL...THERDDY... THERDDY-FIVE... GOODBYE, MR. AVERILL... FORTY...

SINCE WEBSTER WAS A SMALL TOWN, IT WAS VERY EASY FOR A MAN OF TALENT...SUCH AS LEM BOONE...TO RISE SWIFTLY! *DILIGENCE*...ONE OF HIS FORTÉS... HELPED GREATLY!

I DREAM O' JEANNIE...WITH THE...LI-I-I-GH-T BROWN HAIR...

THWACK!

WITH EACH SALE, LEM'S REPUTATION INCREASED! THE WORD SPREAD...EVEN TO NEIGHBORING TOWNS! LEM, PRESSED FOR SPACE, HAD TO MOVE TO BIGGER AND BETTER QUARTERS!

'MORNING, MR. BOONE!

LEM BOONE'S WIG EMPORIUM

HOWDY DO, MRS. MILLER!

WEBSTER WAS NO DIFFERENT THAN ANY OTHER TOWN! A TEMPORARY EPIDEMIC OF ROSE FEVER...BIRTHS...DEATHS! AND LEM TOOK MORE THAN A PASSING INTEREST IN FUNERALS!

♪ POOR JUD IS...*DAID!* ♪ POOR JUD...♪

THWACK!

THERE WAS NO DOUBT THAT LEM WAS A MASTER TRADES-MAN! MEN DOFFED THEIR HATS...NEVER KNOWING WHOSE HAIR WAS *REAL*...WHOSE HAIR WAS *LEM'S!* SUCH WAS THE CASE!

PLEASANT DAY, AIN'T IT, FRANK?

RIGHT PLEASANT, HORACE!

3

BUT...ONE DAY...A CUSTOMER ENTERED LEM'S WIG SALON! ONLY THIS ONE WAS DIFFERENT...RADICALLY DIFFERENT! IT HAD NEVER HAPPENED TO LEM BEFORE! IT WAS A...WOMAN!

UH...HOWDY...(GULP)...DO, MISS? YA AIN'T IN THE WRONG PLACE, ARE YA, MA'M? THIS IS LEM BOONE'S RARIFIED...!

YA CAN SETTLE DOWN, MR. BOONE! I KNOW WHERE I'M AT! AND...I KNOW WHAT I CAME FER! A WIG!! FER....ME!

YOU'VE GOT A HUGE REPU-TATION, MR. BOONE! I CAN TRUST YA! I WANT A WIG OF...STRAIGHT...LONG...BLACK....HAIR, MR. BOONE! I WILL PAY ANYTHING FER IT...AS LONG AS I GETS WHAT I WANT! YA SEE...I'M WELL-TO-DO ...VERY WELL-TO-DO, MR. BOONE!

YA FLATTER ME, MA'M! LEM BOONE'S ALWAYS PROUD TA SERVE THE WELL-TO-DO!

YA WON'T GET A PLUG NICKEL...IF YA DON'T SATISFY, MR. BOONE! DON'T FERGET...STRAIGHT LONG BLACK HAIR! GOOD-BYE, MR. BOONE!

NUFF SAID! YA'LL BE DOO-LY SAT-IS-FIED, MA'M! TAKE MY WORD FER IT!

HERE WAS A REAL CHOPPING GOOD CHANCE FOR LEM...AND HE HAD PLANNED TO EXECUTE IT IN THE USUAL WAY! HE WENT TO THE CEMETERY...FOUND THE SHOVEL...DUG...BUT...

OH, LOVELY TA LOOK...HUH?! THET...AIN'T LONG BLACK HAIR! GOT TA FIND IT...IN ANUTHER PLACE!

EXCITEDLY, LEM WIELDED HIS SPADE AGAIN, UN-COVERING ANOTHER GRAVE! BEADS OF SWEAT DOTTED HIS BROW! THERE WAS NOTHING! HE TRIED ONCE MORE! NOTHING...

WHAT'S GOIN' ON HEAH?!! I JES'...CAIN'T FIND THET STYLE HAIR!

ONCE MORE HE DUG! FAILURE! AND AGAIN...FAILURE! HIS BACK ACHED...AND HE LEFT BEHIND HIM A TRAIL OF COFFINS AS HE LEFT THE CEMETERY AND ENTERED THE PRAIRIE!

THE MOON-LIT PRAIRIE WAS WIDE AND EMPTY! LEM HAD USED UP HIS STORE OF GRAVES...NOTHING SEEMED TO BE LEFT! HE HAD JUST ABOUT GIVEN UP HOPE...WHEN...

JIMINY-HOSEPHAT! THET GRAVE...COULD IT BE? IT'S MY...LAST CHANCE ...NOHOW!

4

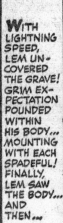

WITH LIGHTNING SPEED, LEM UNCOVERED THE GRAVE! GRIM EXPECTATION POUNDED WITHIN HIS BODY... MOUNTING WITH EACH SPADEFUL! FINALLY, LEM SAW THE BODY... AND THEN...

♪...GET YA IN A TAXI... HONEY!♪

THWACK!

SO....LATER THAT NIGHT...

MR. BOONE, YOU'RE A TRUE CRAFTS-MAN! I AM COMPLETELY....AND OVERWHELMINGLY...SATISFIED! NAME YOUR PRICE, MR. BOONE... AN' IT'S YOUR'N!

I'M NOT ONE TA BANDY A-BOUT, MADAME! PRICE AIN'T NO OBJECT! I'LL JES' SEND MY TAB IN THE YOO-NITED STATES MAIL!

IT WAS A HAPPY, FULL WEEK FOR LEM BOONE! HE SMILED OVER IT... IN HIS DIMLY LIT BACKROOM ~ HUMMING A PLAINTIVE MELODY...OBLIVIOUS TO ANYTHING...AND ANYONE!

♪...DO DO THET VOODOO...♪ THET YOU DO TA ME...♪

WAS IT THE SILENCE THAT MADE LEM TURN AROUND? WAS IT THE HORROR THAT WAS BEFORE HIM... THAT MADE HIM SCREAM? WAS IT DEATH THAT HE FACED? ALL ANSWERED...YES!

WHA--T? GIT...AWAY... FUM ME! NO... NO...

THEN CAME A FAMILIAR SOUND... A FAMILIAR SIGHT...A FAMILIAR ACTION! BUT... LEM BOONE KNEW... IT WAS REVERSED...AS HE HEARD THE SCRAPING SOUND OF HIS HAIR SHORN FROM HIS HEAD!

WHO...STOLE MY HEART...AWAY? WHO...?!! ♪♪

THWACK!

HE....MAKE-UM ME BALD! IS NOT RIGHT... FOR GERONIMO! SO....I TAKE-UM HIS... HAIR! YOU BETCHUM.

THE END

DOOMSDAY

The night watchman at the Tower Art Gallery, elderly Thomas Gainor, turned the powerful beam of his flashlight up and down the corridor, revealing nothing but dignified emptiness. Gainor nodded, clicked the flash shut, and shuffled into the exhibition hall. His hand hovered at the light switch, then reluctantly moved away. No use antagonizing the boss.

The crowds had long since gone, and the gallery was dim and deserted. Even the echoes of the critics' excited, enthusiastic babble of acclaim for the artist were finally stilled. The mantle of midnight had fallen, shrouding in merciful darkness the walls of the Tower Art Gallery and the paintings by William Damon which hung upon them.

" . . . fiercely unconventional," the morning newspapers would say . . . "strange, darkly sinister subjects executed by a master hand" . . . "a great new talent, bringing something new and deeply disturbing to the American art scene . . ."

"But nobody ever said I couldn't shine my flash on the paintings!" the old man chortled silently. The harsh yellow beam played over the nearest one, a screaming study in scarlet, called simply "HELL." Gainor shuddered. Was this what modern art was coming to? The next one was even worse. A huge mottled blob of a face—undistinguishable as male or female — writhing and twisting in abject, consuming terror. Its name was "ECSTASY." It made the night watchman a little sick to his stomach.

By the time he reached the last one, the flashlight in Gainor's hand wavered noticeably. But it never occurred to him not to look. And this time he gasped aloud at what he saw. Against a background of roaring flames and toppling buildings, all the demons of eternity leered out at him from the canvas, their faces grinning monstrosities of joy at the total destruction around them. Only one face was not smiling — the face of a young, incredibly lovely girl who gazed up in horror at the demons from the pile of rubble on which she lay. The brass name-plate at the bottom of the painting read "DOOMSDAY."

. . . "it's pretty terrible, isn't it?" a girl's voice said quietly in the darkness . . . "to know that's what doomsday will be like . . ."

The old man spun around with surprising agility. "Who's there?" he croaked. The beam of his flashlight knifed through the dimness and encircled the slim figure of a girl who stood gazing pensively out the window. "What are you doing here, Miss?" he demanded shakily.

The girl didn't turn around, and when she spoke, her voice was dreamy. "I'm sorry if I startled you, sir," she said quietly. "I stayed after everyone else had gone this afternoon. I wanted to be alone with my face this one last time. You see, I was William Damon's model. It's my face he stole for that painting . . ."

"You make it sound as though he actually took your face off you and put it in the picture!" Gainor interrupted crossly.

. . . the girl turned around . . . "but that's exactly what I do mean," she said simply out of the empty space where her face should have been . . .

BE **WITCHED** EVERY MONTH!

DON'T MISS A SINGLE ISSUE OF...

WITCHES TALES

Special Offer $1⁰⁰

12 ISSUES

WITCHES TALES
1860 BROADWAY
NEW YORK 23, N.Y.

CHECK ☒

| 12 ISSUES $1.00 | 25 ISSUES $2.00 |

ENCLOSED IS $_____ AGE ☐
ZORTHL MAGAZINES CHICAGO

PRINT NAME _____

ADDRESS _____

CITY _____

ZONE _____ STATE _____

SORRY. NO SUBSCRIPTIONS OUTSIDE OF U. S. A.

Mother Mongoose's NURSERY CRIMES

A FARMER WENT TROTTING ON HIS GRAY MARE, BUMPETY, BUMPETY, BUMP!

WITH HIS DAUGHTER BEHIND HIM, SO ROSY AND FAIR, NO RIGGETY-RAGGETY SHLUMP!

A SALESMAN CRIED "STOP!" AND BOTH LOOKED AROUND, STUMPETY, STUMPETY, STUMP!

FROM BEGINNING TO END, HE WAS VERY TIGHTLY BOUND, CLUMPETY, CLUMPETY, CLUMP!

Mother Mongoose's NURSERY CRIMES

"SEE A PIN AND PICK IT UP,

ALL THE DAY YOU'LL HAVE GOOD LUCK!

SEE A PIN AND LET IT LIE,

YOU'LL WISH YOU'D NEVER PASSED IT BY!"

MISS CHEPPER POLITELY WATCHED HER BOSS, MR. CRAVEN, TRUNDLE OUT THE OFFICE... ATTENTIVELY HEARD HIS FOOTSTEPS DIE OUT... THEN RETURNED TO THE SWITCHBOARD TELEPHONE!

HULLO, RACHEL? STILL THERE? YEAH, THAT WAS CRAVEN, WHAT? AW, WHO PAYS ATTENTION TA *HIM*? HE'S *NOTHIN'*! YEAH! I... UH... HOLD IT A SEC, WILL YA, RACHEL? THERE'S SOMETHING HERE...

DAILY NEWS

MADMAN ON TH... LOOSE AS TH... GIRL IS SLA...

POLICE SEEK KILLE... ADMIT NO CLUES

RACHEL! I JUST READ THE NOOS-PAPER! YEAH! YOU, TOO? A GIRL AIN'T *SAFE* NO MORE, ALREADY! I'M TELLIN' YA -- SORT OF GIVES ME THE CREEPY-WEEPIES! WHAT? YA GOTTA HANG UP? OKAY, RACHEL-- DIG YA NOW... CALL YA LATER! TA-TAAA!

AFTER DONA TURNED THE LEVER KEY ON THE SWITCHBOARD ENDING HER CALL, THE SILENCE SEEMED TO BE DEAFENING! SHE QUICKLY READ THE STORY... RAVENOUSLY DEVOURING ALL THE SORDID DETAILS!

SHE FINISHED THE ACCOUNT... LEANED BACK IN HER CHAIR... AND BEGAN TO THINK! THE OFFICE WAS EMPTY! SHE WAS ALONE... AND IT WAS NIGHT! THEN... SHE FINGERED THE SWITCH-BOARD DIAL!

GOTTA TAWK TA SOMEBODY! I'LL GO OUTTA MY HEAD, IF I DON'! MAYBE... EMMA'S HOME?

HULLO, EMMA! MAN O' MAN.... AM I GLAD TO TAWK TA YOU! YOU'LL NEVER KNOW HOW MUCH! SO, SPEAK TA ME, ALREADY! I'M ALL *ALONE* IN THE OFFICE... AND...

DONA CHEPPER BEGAN TO TALK AGAIN... NOT ABOUT ANY-THING IN PARTICULAR... BUT ABOUT THIS AND THAT! ANY-THING TO HEAR HERSELF! SUDDENLY, SHE SWIRLED TO A HARD KNOCKING ON THE DOOR!

YEAH... YEAH! OOOO! HOLD IT, EMMA... *SOMEBODY'S AT THE DOOR! DON'T HANG UP!* STAY... WHERE YA ARE! IF YA HEAR ME SCREAM.... *RUN FOR THE NEAREST COP!* I'LL BE... DEAD!

KNOCK KNOCK

2

DONA STOOD MUTE, WATCHING THE CLOSED DOOR! OR WAS IT SHUT? A CRACK OF LIGHT SEEPED INTO THE ROOM! IT WAS OPENED...AND A SHADOW CREPT ACROSS THE OFFICE!

A MAN ENTERED...A MAN DONA NEVER SAW BEFORE...A MAN DRESSED IN WORK CLOTHES...CARRYING A BLACK SATCHEL...A WILD GLINT IN HIS EYES... A LEER THAT CUT INTO HIS FACE!

I'M FROM THE TELEPHONE COMPANY! HEE! HEE! WE GOT WORD THAT YOUR PHONE'S... OUT OF ORDER! YOU KNOW...LIKE A STEADY BZZ-BZZZ COMING OVER IT! YEAH...A BZZ-BZZZ! HEE! HEE!

NO! THE PHONE'S AWRIGHT! N-NOTHIN'S WRONG! IT WORKS ...FINE!

HA!! THAT'S A HOT ONE! A REAL...DOOZY! DO YOU THINK THE COMPANY'LL SEND ME DOWN...IF THE PHONE WAS OKAY? HA!! NOT ON YOUR...UH... LIFE! YOUR PHONE'S OUT OF ORDER! THAT'S...FINAL!

HIS HYSTERICAL LAUGHTER ECHOED THROUGH THE OFFICE! DONA HEARD IT BOUND OFF THE FOUR WALLS ...AS HE CAME TOWARDS HER...FORCING HER AGAINST THE SWITCHBOARD!

B-BUT....IT WORKS, IT...WORKS ...FINE! BELIEVE ME, ALREADY! OH, GO...AWAY! PLEASE! I'M ...ALL ALONE!

DON'T I....KNOW ...IT! HEE!

DONA COULDN'T GO BACK ANY FURTHER! SHE WAS BACKED UP... AND THERE WAS ONLY ONE PLACE TO GO...FORWARD! WITH A LURCH, SHE BOLTED...PASSED THE MAN...

DON'T... TOUCH ...ME!!!

WHERE ARE YOU GOING, LADY? DON'T... RUN!!!

YOU'RE A REAL CORKER, LADY! I LIKE YOUR SENSE OF HUMOR! BUT... WHERE ARE YOU RUNNING? THERE'S...NO PLACE...TO GO!

HEY! DID YOU READ ABOUT THAT MURDERER? THEY SAY HE'S A REAL MANIAC! KILLIN' WOMEN...LIKE THAT! ALWAYS GETTING THEM...ALONE... WHEN THEY'RE... DEFENSELESS... EXACTLY LIKE YOU ARE NOW!

OH, WHAT D' YA WANT... ALREADY?! WHY DON'CHA LEMME... ALONE? GO...'WAY, PLEASE!

4

Men! Send for This Money-Making Outfit FREE!

See How Easy It Is to Make UP TO $15.00 IN A DAY!

Do you want to make more money in full or spare time . . . as much as $15.00 in a day? Then mail the coupon below for this BIG OUTFIT, sent you FREE, containing more than 150 fine quality fabrics, sensational values in made-to-measure suits, topcoats, and overcoats. Take orders from friends, neighbors, fellow-workers. Every man prefers better-fitting, better-looking made-to-measure clothes, and when you show the many beautiful, high quality fabrics—mention the low prices for made-to-measure fit and style—and show our guarantee of satisfaction, you take orders right and left. You collect a big cash profit in advance on every order, and build up fine permanent income for yourself in spare or full time.

YOUR OWN SUITS WITHOUT 1¢ COST!

Our plan makes it easy for you to get your own personal suits, topcoats, and overcoats without paying 1¢—in addition to your big cash earnings. Think of it! Not only do we start you on the road to making big money, but we also make it easy for you to get your own clothes without paying one penny. No wonder thousands of men write enthusiastic letters of thanks.

Just Mail Coupon

You don't invest a penny of your money now or any time. You don't pay money for samples, for outfits, or for your own suit under our remarkable plan. So do as other men have done—mail the coupon now. Don't send a penny. Just send us the coupon.

NO EXPERIENCE NEEDED

It's amazingly easy to take measures, and you don't need any experience to take orders. Everything is simply explained for you to cash in on this wonderful opportunity. Just mail this coupon now and we'll send you this big, valuable outfit filled with more than 150 fine fabrics and everything else you need to start. You'll say this is the greatest way to make money you ever saw. Rush the coupon today!

PROGRESS TAILORING CO., Dept. E-276
500 S. Throop Street, Chicago 7, Illinois

Progress Tailoring Co., Dept. E-276
500 S. Throop St., Chicago 7, Illinois

Dear Sir: I WANT MONEY AND I WANT A SUIT TO WEAR AND SHOW, without paying 1¢ for it. Rush Valuable Suit Coupon and Sample Kit with actual fabrics ABSOLUTELY FREE.

Name_____ Age_____

Address_____

City_____ State_____

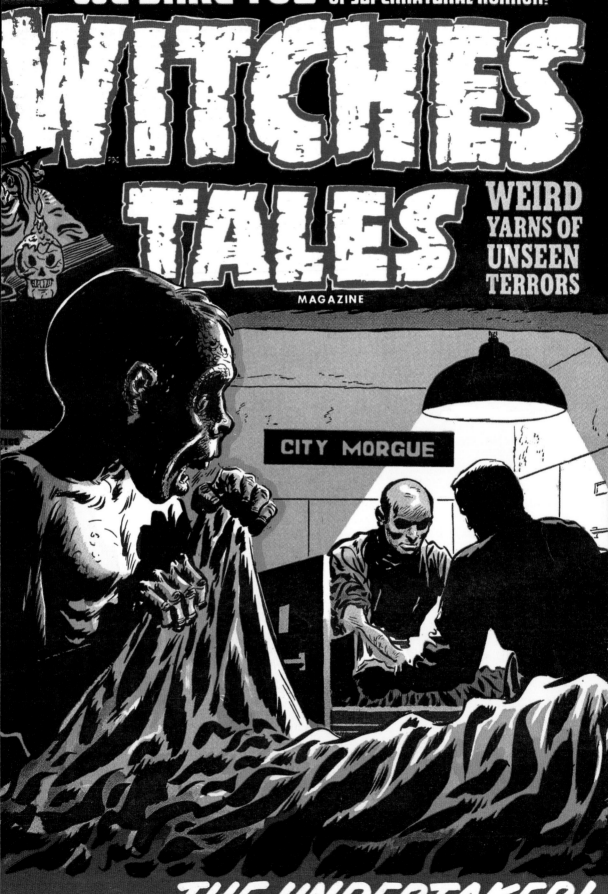

WITCHES TALES, APRIL, 1954, VOL. 1, NO. 24, IS PUBLISHED BI-MONTHLY by WITCHES TALES, INC., 1860 Broadway, New York 23, N.Y. Entered as second class matter at the Post Office at New York, N.Y., under the Act of March, 3, 1879. Single copies, 10c. Subscription rates, 10 issues for $1.00 in the U. S. and possessions, elsewhere $1.50. All names in this periodical are entirely fictitious and no identification with actual persons is intended. Contents copyrighted, 1954, by Witches Tales, Inc., New York, City. Printed in the U.S.A. Title registered in U. S. Patent Office.

The four greatest weird books, in announcing a new policy, have pulled one of the most terrifying coup d'etats in the sanctified realm of horror.

For, CHAMBER OF CHILLS, WITCHES TALES, TOMB OF TERROR, and BLACK CAT MYSTERY have joined together in a four-power horror pact.

And this package of unbeatable shock will come to you in a cyclical pattern of doom, with four distinctive terror books getting to you during a two-month period. Thus, a mag belonging to this group will appear on your newsstands every two weeks -- each one a king of shock.

Just look at this shock king's domain...

BLACK CAT MYSTERY will offer you a package of real-life horror, where man meets man in a mad clash of reality...

WITCHES TALES is designed to tickle your funny bone and chill your spine, the strangest and most different terror mag ever created.

TOMB OF TERROR will consist of stories told out of this world, an unmistakeable unit of horror ripped from the many unexplored voids...

CHAMBER OF CHILLS will carry you to the incredible sphere of the supernatural whose teller is as weird as his stories!

Look for them!

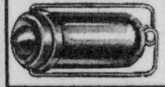

PA HAS TOLD ME A LOT!
HE'S TOLD ME THAT THE WORLD
OUTSIDE IS HARD...CRUEL... ROTTEN
TO THE CORE! HE'S ALSO TOLD ME
TO STAY AS FAR AWAY FROM
IT AS I CAN. THEREBY
HANGS A TALE!
YOU SEE...

I...LIKE...
IT...
OUTSIDE...!

DOXY!

So...for all my life...my whole world was confined to an undertaking parlor! Can you imagine such a world? Age-worn carpets...continual silence...dead bodies...swathed with rigor-mortis...being rolled to a waiting coffin...

...dressed in Sunday's finest...hands clasped angelically...reposing on a bed of wood...soft satin ruffled to caress its face...

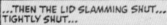

...then the lid slamming shut...tightly shut...

SLAM!

RRRRRMMMM

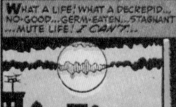

What a life! What a decrepid...no-good...germ-eaten...stagnant...mute life! I can't...

...take it...

...any more...!

WHAM

3

BUT, PA, I'M NOT A YOUNG KID! I WANT TO GET OUT! I...FEEL... STIFLED!

STIFLED, IS IT? LOOK TO THYSELF, CHILD! SEARCH YOUR SOUL! CLEANSE YOUR HEART ...OF TEMPTATION!

OUTSIDE ARE THE FIRES! THEIR ANGRY LICKS REACH OUT TO CONSUME YOU! BEWARE, CHILD! DO NOT GO INTO THE WORLD!

STAY WITH ME, MY SON! HERE -- IN THE SAFETY OF DEATH! HERE... WHERE THERE ARE NOT THE PITFALLS OF CARNAL THIRST! STAY, DOXY! STAY..!

I CAN'T STAY, THOUGH! I'M FED UP! I'M LEAVING... *HAHAHA*... AND PA WON'T KNOW A THING... BECAUSE I'VE GOT A PLAN...

IT'S PERFECT... SOMETHING PA WILL NEVER SUSPECT... YET... *HEEHEE*... IT'LL HAPPEN RIGHT UNDER HIS BIG, FAT, ROSY NOSE...

NOW... ALL I HAVE TO DO IS PUT IT INTO ACTION... *HAHAHA* AND... *I'LL BE AS FREE AS A BIRD...*

IT'S

SO...

SIMPLE...

4

I LAY IN THE COFFIN...QUIET...HUSHED...STILL! NO MUSCLE WITHIN ME STIRRED! PA CALLED TO ME...

DOXYYYY! YOO HOO! THIS...COFFIN'S GOT...TO GO! DOXYYYY!

PA COULDN'T FIND ME! HE DID ALL THE WORK BY HIMSELF...NOT KNOWING HOW CLOSE I WAS TO HIM...

WHERE...IS...THAT...CHILD?

WE'RE OFF! SOON AS WE...HAHAHA...GET TO THE CEMETERY...AND PA DELIVERS THIS COFFIN...

...I'LL BREAK OUT OF THIS COFFIN...AND...RUN LIKE A BEAVER...FREE...HEEHEEHEE...I'LL BE FREE...

ONLY...

I FORGOT...

THE FIRES...

CREMATORIUM

THE END

PICTURES

Driblets of clouds floated by the moon, casting the street in moving, dark shadows. Harry Peck waited, fingering the camera ever so slightly. *They're still talking . . .*

He inched forward, out of the building's protective corner, coming nearer the opened window. *Get it right,* Peck thought, *snap it when they plunge the knife into him!*

Peck was out in the open now, standing immediately in front of the window; he held the camera to his eye. He saw the three figures: the sleeping man, the blonde woman with her fiendish gleam, and the other man, his face broken out in beads of glistening sweat, gripping the knife.

Suddenly, the knife fell. Peck snapped the shutter. There was the grating sound of steel into flesh, followed by a throaty death grunt. Then, Peck ran, away from the house, away from the murder; he ran, his breath coming hard. He held the camera tightly in his hand, not wanting to lose it now . . . not after he got his picture.

Then, he stopped, resting his frame against a tree. It was quiet, the air about him hushed and still. *No good,* he thought. Peck wasn't satisfied. *The boss wouldn't like it.* He had to have the right one . . . with the right tone . . . with the right spirit! "Real gore!" that's what the boss said.

He took out a cigarette, lit a match and, out of the corner of his eye, caught a glimpse of a woman in the middle of a street. She was alone. *Too alone!* Instinctively, Peck shot the camera to his eye level and caught the woman in its square sights.

I knew it! Another murder! The woman was trapped in the glare of a car's headlights, webbed inescapably in the twin orbs of the machine-monster that bore down on her with the speed of a death projectile.

Peck caught the action. The car hit the woman head-on, sending her tumbling to the the floor and then, in a clash of gears, zooming on. The woman lay on the ground, her head smashed in a pool of blood. She was dead.

Peck was dejected, though. *It's not what I want. Not what the boss wants! Gore . . . real, ugly, horrible gore . . . !* He felt despondent, walking along the residential street.

Abruptly, he shivered. His spine tingled. The cold, clammy, invisible hand of fear tore across his face, leaving him frozen to the spot he was standing at. He stared wide-eyed at the scene before him.

. . . . T-there it is! He slowly lifted the camera, his fingers twisted with fright. *God, how horrible!* His tongue felt as though it was swollen as he licked his lips. *Get it over with . . . and run!* Peck snapped the shutter.

Later, Peck flung the finished, glossy photographs on his boss's desk.

The boss looked at them, wincing. "Yeow!" The boss shuddered. "That's what I want!"

Peck smiled. "Yeah," he said, "I knew you'd like it. Nothing so horrible to us . . . like CHILDREN PLAYING!"

The boss looked at Peck. They both smiled. Peck and his boss were ghouls, ugly, torn ghouls — and pictures of children playing, for ghouls, are real gore.

STATEMENT OF THE OWNERSHIP, MANAGEMENT AND CIRCULATION REQUIRED BY THE ACT OF CONGRESS OF AUGUST 24, 1912, AS AMENDED BY THE ACTS OF MARCH 3, 1933, AND JULY 2, 1946, OF WITCHES TALES published Monthly at New York, N. Y.' for October 1, 1953.

1. The names and addresses of the publisher, editor, managing editor, and business managers are: Editor: Leon Harvey, 1860 Broadway, N. Y. C.; Managing Editor: Alfred Harvey, 1860 Broadway, N. Y. C.; Business Manager: Robert B. Harvey, 1860 Broadway, N. Y. C. Publisher: Witches Tales, Inc. 1860 Broadway, N. Y. C.

2. The owners are Witches Tales, Inc. , 1860 Broadway, N. Y. C.; Leon Harvey, 1860 Broadway, N. Y. C.; Alfred Harvey, 1860 Broadway, N. Y. C.; Robert B. Harvey, 1860 Broadway, N. Y. C.

3. The known bondholders, mortgagees, and other security holders owning or holding 1 percent or more of total amount of bonds, mortgages, or other securities are: None.

4. Paragraphs 2 and 3 include, in cases where the stockholder or security holder appears upon the books of the company as trustee or in any other fiduciary relation, the name of the person or corporation for whom such trustee is acting; also the statements in the two paragraphs show the affiant's full knowledge and belief as to the circumstances and conditions under which stockholders and security holders who do not appear upon the books of the company as trustees, hold stock and securities in a capacity other than that of a bona fide owner.

(signed) ROBERT B. HARVEY, Business Manager

Sworn and subscribed to before me this 30th day of September, 1953.
Moe J. Mascheroni (My commission expires March 30th, 1954)

"PUSSY CAT, PUSSY CAT WHERE HAVE YOU BEEN?"

SAID THE CAT - "I'VE GONE TO SEE ONE OF MY KIN!"

"PUSSY CAT, PUSSY CAT, HAS YOUR KIN A NAME?"

"NO." SAID THE CAT, "BUT I LIKE HIM ALL THE SAME!"

DOCTOR FOSTER WENT TO GLOUCESTER

IN A TORRENT OF RAIN! THE BRIDGE - IT HAD TUMBLED,

THE HORSE - IT HAD FUMBLED, SO DOCTOR FOSTER

NEVER WENT TO GLOUCESTER AGAIN!

NOW WE GO TO THE BOOK-SHELF AND PULL OUT ONE OF THE WORLD'S MOST FAMOUS STORIES, AND SHOW YOU HOW *WITCHES TALES* WOULD DO IT!

MUTINY ON THE BOUNDARY

THE HMS *BOUNDARY*, BOUND FOR TAHITI AND THE SOUTH SEAS, WAS A TOMB OF TORTURE FOR ITS MEN -- FOR RULING WITH AN IRON FIST AND A BLACK SOUL WAS ITS POWER-CRAZED CAPTAIN, THE TYRANT, WILLIAM BLAH!

MITH-TER GOBBLE! THAT IS *HOW* WE *MUST DEAL* WITH THESE *CURTH*, AS MY *FIRST MATE* -- *YOU SHOULD* HAVE DEALT OUT PROPER *PUNISHMENT!*

BUT, SIR! THE MAN HAS NOT BEEN WELL FOR TWO DAYS NOW. HE COULDN'T HAVE TURNED THE WHEEL MUCH MORE QUICKLY--

DLEATH DO NOT TAKE *ITH-THUE* WITH MY *ORDER-TH*, MITH-TER GOBBLE! I AM *STILL CAPTAIN* OF THITH *SHIP!* I SHALL NOT BE THITH LENIENT WITH *ANY* OF *THESE MEN* AGAIN. I AM THE *LAW* HERE. I MUST BE *OBEYED*-- TO THE *LETTER!*

YES, CAPTAIN!

DAY AFTER DAY.. HOUR AFTER HOUR.. A RAVING, RANTING MADMAN STRODE UP AND DOWN 'THE DECKS, HOLDING THE POWER OF LIFE OVER A HUNDRED TERROR-STRICKEN, SULLEN MEN...

THITH BRATH-RAILING IS *FILTHY*, THCUM! YOU *HAVE NOT CARRIED* OUT MY ORDERTH! DO YOU *KNOW* THE *PENALTY* FOR SUCH *CARE-LETHNETH!* *DEATH!* *YETH!* I CAN *PRONOUNCE* DEATH ON YOU! MITHTER GOBBLE! MITHTER GOB-BLE!

HERE, CAPTAIN. BEGGING THE CAPTAIN'S PARDON-- BUT WON'T YOU HAVE *PITY* AND *COMMUTE* HIS SENTENCE, SIR?

PERHAPTH YOU ARE RIGHT! WE HAVE NEED OF ALL HANDTH! UP, THWINE -- YOU'LL HANG BY THE YARD-ARM INSTEAD!

NO! N-NO! PLEASE, CAP'N.. PLEASE--! NOT THAT! I--I'LL BE DEAD BY MORNIN'!

NO! NO...UGH! NO-O-O-O..!

LIFT HIM *HIGHER*... THERE! LET HIM *FEEL* THE *WIND* ON HITH *TREMBLING* FACE!

YOU *DIRTY*... *FAT DOG!* MAY YOU *ROT* IN *HADES* FOR YOUR *BLACK HEART!*

YOU DARE THPEAK BACK TO ME? MITHTER GOBBLE! CLAP THIS ROGUE IN IRONS! WE SHALL TAKE HIM BACK TO ENGLAND FOR HANGING!

RISE UP! CRUSH THIS *CRAZED* HOUND, LADS! UP... AT... HIM...!

BLAH LISTENED TO THE SCREAMING SAILOR- CALMLY LISTENED AS HE WIPED HIS BROW-CALMLY LISTENED, AS A TIC IN THE CORNER OF HIS EYE BOTHERED HIM- CALMLY LISTENED, AS HE WITHDREW A FLINTLOCK FROM HIS BELT-AND FIRED...

THE BALL ENTERED THE SAILOR WITH A SUDDEN THUD,...TOPPLING HIM OVER,...DEAD! BLAH BREATHED HEAVILY A FEW TIMES - AND THEN TURNED TOWARDS HIS FIRST MATE...

CLEAR THE *DECK* OF THITH... *CARRION*, MITHTER GOBBLE! WE *SHALL NOT* THTAND FOR *INTHUBORDINATION* ON THITH *SHIP!* FOLLOW ME OUT, THIR!

2

NIGHT CAME AND WITH IT, SURCEASE! CAPTAIN BLAH RETIRED TO HIS CABIN AFTER A HEARTY MEAL... AND SLEPT SOUNDLY! MEANWHILE...A FEW MEN SPOKE IN HUSHED WHISPERS...THEIR FACES LIT BY PALE LANTERN LIGHT...

HEAR ME OUT, HUGH. WE MUST KILL HIM! WE CANNOT CONTINUE UNDER HIS WILL MUCH LONGER!

LOWER...YOUR VOICE, LAD! HMM! AYE... 'TIS THE BEST WAY!

NO, JAMIE. 'TIS THE WRONG WAY--BECAUSE IT IS MUTINY! HAVE PATIENCE! WE SHALL FIND HARBOR AT TAHITI SOON.

TAHITI--SONG--WOMEN FOR ALL OF US! HAPPINESS-- LAUGHTER..AY--IT IS LIKE A DREAM OF HEAVEN. ALL RIGHT, HUGH... WE'LL WAIT!

YES..WE MUST WAIT...WAIT!

THE MEN BIDED THEIR TIME... SAVORING THE SWEET DREAM OF REACHING A MISTY ISLAND... CRANING THEIR NECKS TOWARDS THE CROW'S NEST WHERE THE FIRST WORD WOULD COME FROM! THEN IT CAME... AND WHEN THE "BOUNDARY" DROPPED ANCHOR...!

ALL LEAVES ARE CANTHELLED, MITHTER GOBBLE! THESE MEN ARE CONFINED TO THEIR QUARTERTH... FOR THEIR THURLY THLIPSHOD DITHOBEDIENCE! I AM GOING ASHORE...TO PRETHENT MY CREDENTIALS!

A-AYE, SIR...!

BUT NEWS OF THE BOUNDARY'S APPEARANCE HAD REACHED THE NATIVES, AND SOON...

PLENTY OF WINE, FOOD, AND SPICES, LADS. STOCK UP BEFORE HIS ROYAL LOWNESS RETURNS! YAHHAOOO!

BUT AS FATE WOULD HAVE IT, CAPTAIN BLAH RETURNED PRE-MATURELY, AND...

THIS IS RANK INTHUBORDINANCE, MITHTER GOBBLE! I HOLD YOU RETHPONTHIBLE FOR THIS SHOCKING OCCURENTH! YOU SHALL BE DOCKED THIX MONTHS PAY..ATH FOR THE RETHT--THE LEMONS...FRUIT... AND FOODSTUFFS....ALL ARE TO BE CATHT OVERBOARD!

BUT, CAPTAIN BLAH..SIR.. WE NEED LEMONS BADLY. SCURVY MAY BREAK OUT.. AND--

THILENTH! I AM WELL AWARE OF THAT! HOWEVER, ORDERTH ARE TO TRANTHPORT POTTED PALMS BACK TO ENGLAND. WE HAVE NO ROOM FOR...LEMONS!

BUT...FOR DARING TO QUESTION MY AUTHORITY...YOU WILL BE PLACED IN THE BRIG ON...BREAD AND WATER...FOR THE DURATION OF OUR VOYAGE! OUT OF MY THIGHT! I AM SHACKLED WITH STUPID FOOLS!

THE DAY OF RECKONING WILL COME, BLAH! I SWEAR IT!

NOW BEGAN THE LONG VOYAGE HOME...AND BLAH GREW INCREASINGLY WORSE...

LAY ON, YOU DECK LICE! MARK WELL YOUR ENERGIES! I'LL *NOT* HAVE A *LAZY MAN* ON BOARD THITH SHIP! *LAY..ON..*

HEAVE... *HEAVE...*

WE CAN *THROW* HIM *OVERBOARD* AND SET *COURSE* FOR THE ISLANDS, HUGH. HE'LL *KILL* US ALL *BEFORE* THIS TRIP'S *FINISHED!*

NO, JAMIE! I HAVE A *BETTER* IDEA. HAVE PATIENCE, MAN.. AND... WAIT... WAIT..!

ONE WEEK LATER, AS THE *BOUNDARY* NEARED THE STORM-TOSSED ARCHIPELAGOS...

YOU *DATHTARDLY* FOOL! I'LL *TEACH* YOU TO POLISH MY BOOTS WITH VIGOR FROM NOW ON. MITHTER GOBBLE... MITHTER GOBBLE I *WANT* THIS MAN *LASHED* TO THE *WHEEL!*

SPARE ME, SIR! THE WIND *WILL* CUT ME TO *RIBBONS!*

THEN THAT *WILL* BE TO YOUR *DITHADVANTAGE*, MY *JACKANAPETH!* WELL! WHAT ARE YOU *THWABIES THTARING* AT ME FOR? GET *ABOUT* YOUR WORK! HALF FOOD RATIONS FOR *ALL*, MITHTER GOBBLE!

DID YOU *HEAR?* MITHTER GOBBLE! ANSWER ME, SIR... AT ONCE! GIVE THE ORDER FOR THESE DECK THCUM TO DITHPERTH! *AT...ONCE...THIR--* OR BY HEAVEN, I'LL ...

MITHTER GOBBLE...DO YOUR *DUTY!* I'M... *CAPTAIN*...HERE! YOU MEN...GO *BACK*.. I'LL HAVE...YOU ALL *HANGED*...FOR M-MUTINY...

AND NOW...AS IF SHOT OUT OF A CANNON, THE HMS *BOUNDARY* SURGED FORWARD LIKE A SOARING BIRD, SWIFTLY AND BUOYANTLY TOWARD HOME...

LAY TO, MATIES! CAPTAIN BLAH HAS GIVEN US A *FULL ROUND* OF *GROG* TONIGHT!

YOUR ORDERS ARE TO RAISE SAIL? AYE...AYE...SIR!

TWO DEGREES NOR' BY NOR'WES', CAPTAIN! WE'RE... *STRAIGHT*...ON COURSE!

AND FOUR MONTHS LATER-- ENGLAND!

I AM LORD TREWAINE, GENTLEMEN... COMMISSIONER OF HIS HIGHNESS' HARBOR! WE HAVE *RECEIVED* A *LETTER* BY *CLIPPER SHIP* FROM YOUR CAPTAIN BLAH...WHILE IN *TAHITI*...THAT HE FEARS *MUTINY* ON BOARD SHIP! *PREPARE* TO STAND INSPECTION!

MUTINY IS A *SERIOUS* OFFENSE, GENTLEMEN. IF CAPTAIN BLAH'S *CHARGES SHOULD PROVE* TO BE *MERITED*...YOU MUST *STAND TRIAL* FOR *TREASON!* I DO NOT SEE HIM. WHERE IS HE?

THERE IS *SOME MISTAKE!* THE CAPTAIN HAS HAD A *SUCCESSFUL VOYAGE.* HE HAS BEEN WITH US *CONSTANTLY!*

AYE, THAT HE HAS, SIR! BY YON *MIZZEN-MAST* HE *WAITS* TO *RECEIVE* YOU!

WE HAVE ALWAYS OBEYED HIS ORDERS--AND NOT ONCE HAVE WE GONE AGAINST HIM.

NOR *HAS* HE HAD ONE *PERVERSE* WORD TO SAY *ABOUT* US, SIR. AND WE *HAVE* CARRIED OUT EVERY *COMMAND* TO THE LETTER! HE HAS *REMAINED* ON THE *QUARTER DECK*--IN *FULL CHARGE.* THERE HAS BEEN...NO *MUTINY*...WAS THERE, CAPTAIN?

FOR THERE STOOD THE TERRIBLE, THE MIGHTY, THE TYRANT, *CAPTAIN BLAH,* NAILED TO THE MAST IN ALL HIS HORRIBLE GLORY-- WATCHING OVER ALL AS WAS HIS RIGHT--AND AGREEING WITH ALL IN *DEATH* AS HE HAD FOR *FIVE MONTHS!*

THE END

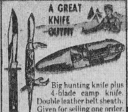

EYE EYE, SIR

ME? I'M RUDY CRANE, PRIVATE DETECTIVE! THE STORY OF MY LIFE IS A SNAPPY TALE. YOU SEE, THEY KICKED ME OUT OF COLLEGE WHEN I WAS ABOUT TWENTY-SEVEN —FOR TRYING TO HAND MISS DUNCAN, MY-BIOLOGY PROF, A COUPLE OF LAUGHS— AFTER SCHOOL...

THE DEAN SAID HE COULDN'T PUT ME BACK IN COLLEGE, BUT I COULD HANG AROUND THE OFFICE AND SWEEP OUT AND WASH WINDOWS. BUT IT WAS NO GO! I WANTED TO BE ON MY OWN—SO I HIT DAD FOR A COUPLE OF MILLION AND OPENED UP THIS SMALL BUT MODEST PRIVATE DICK FIRM! SETTLE BACK AND LISTEN TO MY FIRST CASE! IT'S A REAL PIP...

OUCH!

SHE WAS MY FIRST CUSTOMER, TALL AND THIN, SOMETHING TO LOOK AT AND THINK ABOUT! AS FAR AS I WAS CONCERNED, THERE WAS NO ONE ELSE IN THE ROOM. I PLAYED IT COOL, THOUGH! CASUAL-LIKE I GREETED HER...

WOW! WEE-HOO! ZOWIE! GO...GO..!

HELLO! MY NAME'S LUCY LATOUR!

STILL KEEPING EVERYTHING INSIDE ME LIKE A JACK-IN-THE-BOX, I SEATED HER AND GOT DOWN TO THE BUSINESS OF THE DAY...

YEAH? WHAT CAN I DO FOR YOU? NAME IT AND IT'S YOURS!

LAY OFF BUSTER! I WANT YOU TO FIND MY HUSBAND! I HAVEN'T SEEN HIM SINCE HE WENT FOR A LOAF OF BREAD THREE YEARS AGO! FIND HIM. YOU SEE, I DON'T LIKE STALE BREAD!

HOW COULD YOUR HUSBAND LEAVE SOMETHING LIKE — YOU? HE MUST HAVE BEEN OFF HIS ROCKER! IF IT WASN'T FOR YOUR GLASSES, YOU'D BE A REAL KNOCKOUT! AS IT IS, YOU AREN'T TOO BAD!

NEVER MIND WHY! JUST FIND HIM! MAYBE AFTERWARDS WE CAN PLAY A GAME WE BOTH LIKE!

THAT WAS ENOUGH FOR ME! I CAN TAKE A HINT! THE LAST PLACE LUCY'S HUSBAND WAS SEEN WAS A BAR UP THE BLOCK AND AROUND THE CORNER — A SMALL DIVE THAT EVEN THE COCKROACHES DIDN'T HAVE GUTS TO GO INTO! ANYWAY, WE WENT THERE...

WOW! ZOWIE! ZSA ZSA GABOR! LOVE IT! GO... GO..!

SIMMER DOWN, BUSTER!

THE BARTENDER WAS TOUGH, BUT NOT TOUGH ENOUGH. I HIT HIM. HE WENT DOWN LIKE A STACK OF DISHES. WHEN HE GOT UP, I GRABBED HIM BY THE COLLAR. I WISHED IT WAS HIS THROAT.

WE'RE LOOKING FOR MRS. LATOUR'S HUSBAND! HAVE YOU SEEN HIM?

NO, I AIN'T SEEN HIM! EVEN IF I DID, I WOULDN'T SAY SO!

HOW COULD A GUY LEAVE SOMETHING LIKE THAT? HE MUST HAVE BEEN OFF HIS ROCKER! IF IT WASN'T FOR HER GLASSES SHE'D BE A REAL KNOCKOUT! AS IT IS, SHE ISN'T TOO BAD!

LET'S GO, LUCY! HE DON'T KNOW ANYTHING!

TOO BAD...

2

THE GROWL IN MY STOMACH TOLD ME I WAS HUNGRY. WHEN LUCY BIT ME IN THE EAR, I KNEW SHE WAS TOO! WE FINISHED UP A FILET IN LIKITY-SPLIT TIME. AND RETURNED TO THE BUSINESS OF THE DAY...

FIGHT IT, RUDY, FIGHT IT WITH ALL YOU GOT! FIND MY HUSBAND FIRST! MAYBE THEN..?

YOU'VE GOT GUTS, LUCY, REAL GUTS! HOW COULD A GUY LEAVE YOU!!! IF IT WEREN'T FOR YOUR GLASSES...

IT WAS NO USE! I HAD TO FIND LUCY'S HUSBAND! HE HAD BELONGED TO A MEN'S CLUB, A SLICK PLACE WITH MILE-HIGH CARPETS THAT SUBBED FOR A MAUSOLEUM AT NIGHT. WE WENT THERE. ALL I COULD FIND WAS A DIGNIFIED JOE...

WOW! ZOWIE! WEE WEE WEE! LUCIUS BEEBE! GO...GO...!

GUY'S ON HIS LAST LEGS! HASN'T AN OUNCE OF LIFE LEFT IN HIM!

YOU'RE RIGHT! BUT HE MIGHT BE A LEAD. ASK HIM, RUDY BABY, ASK HIM—FAST!

THE WAY LUCY SPOKE, I KNEW SOMETHING WAS UP! I GAVE THE JOE A SHORT RIGHT UNDER THE HEART. I LIKED IT! IT WAS A GOOD ONE! HE BLUBBERED FOR A WHILE AND QUIETED DOWN. BUT, LIKE I SAID, IT WAS NO USE.

LATOUR? DEVILISH GOOD SORT! REAL BATTLESHIP! MISSING, YOU SAY? RAN OUT ON YOU, EH? BLOODY, INFAMOUS DEED! NO, I HAVEN'T SEEN HIM FOR THREE MONTHS!

IT'S NO GO LUCY! BLOCKED AGAIN!

YES...

WE LEFT! THE CORRIDOR WAS DARK AS WE ENTERED IT! THE OLD GUY WAS TALKING TO HIMSELF. I WANTED TO GIVE HIM A QUICK JAB IN THE TEETH, BUT I CHANGED MY MIND. I HAD OTHER THINGS ON IT!

DEVILISHLY GOOD-LOOKING WOMAN! LATOUR'S WIFE, EH? LEFT HER, TOO! BEYOND ME HOW HE COULD HAVE DONE A THING LIKE THAT! CONFOUNDED BLACKGUARD! TOO BAD ABOUT THOSE GLASSES THOUGH...

LIKE I SAID, THE CORRIDOR WAS DARK. THINGS KEPT RUNNING THROUGH MY BRAIN, THINGS I WANTED TO THINK ABOUT!

SUDDENLY, I GRABBED HER. SHE FELL INTO MY ARMS LIKE AN AIR-FOAM CUSHION. THE SWEET SCENT OF HER PERFUME REMINDED ME OF SPINACH. I HAD TO HAVE HER, SO I KICKED HER IN THE SHINS. I LOVED IT. SHE FOUGHT BACK LIKE A TIGER...

NO, NO...MY HUSBAND'S NOT FOUND. HONEY, NOT YET! NOT YET!

WHACKY, YOU'RE DRIVING ME WHACKY! HOW LONG CAN I WAIT?

3

LUCY LATOUR HAD HER FISH-HOOKS IN ME AND SHE WAS HANGING ON FOR DEAR LIFE. IT HURT BUT I LOVED IT! TRACKING DOWN ALL LEADS, WE WENT TO HER HUSBAND'S PLACE OF BUSINESS. AND IN THE ELEVATOR...

KEEP YOUR EYES STRAIGHT, BUSTER! OR ELSE YOU'LL GET ONE RIGHT IN THE TEETH! YELL OUT THE FIFTEENTH FLOOR!

Y-YES, SIR!

WE STOPPED AT THE FIFTEENTH FLOOR. I RABBIT-PUNCHED THE OPERATOR. IT WAS A GOOD ONE. WE WENT INTO AN OFFICE WITH A DESK AS LONG AS THE WHOLE BAY OF BISCAY. THE JOKER BEHIND IT SLIPPED A SMILE INTO HIS FACE...

WOW! ZOWIE! ZOOM ZOOM ZOOM! ADOLPH MENJOU GO...GO...!

COOL OFF! JUST TELL US WHERE LATOUR IS!

IT WAS THE SAME STORY...

LATOUR! GOOD KID! HARD WORKER. LAST TIME I SAW HIM HE WAS WITH A COP! YOU MEAN TO SAY...!

YEA! YEA! WE KNOW! IF IT WASN'T FOR THE GLASSES...!

I LEFT THE GUY. MY BREATH WAS BATED. THE TRAIL WAS GETTING HOT AND I LIKED THE FLAME. LUCY AND I HOPPED A CAB AND WENT TO THE POLICE STATION. THE PLACE STANK LIKE AN OLD SALAMI. THE STAIRS CREEKED...

WE FINALLY MADE IT! THE OLD SARGEANT, THAT LOOKED TOO MUCH LIKE A WALRUS, CHEWED UP AN OLD CIGAR AS IF IT WAS LICORICE. I WAS ABOUT TO GIVE HIM ONE IN THE GUT WHEN LUCY STOPPED ME. SHE WAS RIGHT! THERE WAS OTHER BUSINESS TO ATTEND TO...

WOW! ZOWIE! RUCKA TUCKA TUCKA!! JIMMY VALENTINE! GO... GO...

DON'T! CONTROL YOURSELF, RUDY!

YEA! MIGHT AS WELL GET DOWN TO BUSINESS!

I ASKED THE WALRUS ABOUT LUCY'S HUSBAND. HE BARKED OUT AN ANSWER THAT SHOCKED EVERYONE PRESENT...

LATOUR? GUY JUST WASHED UP BY THE RIVER FITS HIS DISCRIPTION! COULD BE THE SAME FELLOW! WANNA GO FOR A LOOK-SEE?

ARE YOU KIDDING? LET'S GET MOVING...

4

WE ALL WENT DOWN TO THE RIVER. IT WAS DAMP AND WET! A STIFF WAS WASHED UP ON SHORE! HE LOOKED DEAD, REAL DEAD! I LIKED THAT. WE ALL STOOD AROUND JUST LOOKING. SUDDENLY, LUCY CRIED. THE KID HAD GUTS...

THAT'S HIM! IS HE THE GUY YOU WANT... THE GUY WHO RAN OUT ON YOU?

YES! OH, YES! THAT'S MY HUSBAND! JAMIE-BOY!

JAMIE! WHAT A MONICKER!

THE OLD WALRUS SPOKE...

I GUESS THAT WRAPS UP THE CASE! YOU TWO BETTER GET ALONG!

MIND YOUR OWN BUSINESS, COPPER! DON'T TREAD ON ME! I GOT SOME THINGS TO DO. RIGHT, LUCY?

I REMEMBER, RUDY!

WE WATCHED THE OLD WALRUS WADDLE AWAY. MY MIND WAS ON OTHER THINGS. LUCY LOOKED INTO MY EYES ...AND SMILED...

HOW COULD A GUY JUMP WHEN HE WAS MARRIED TO SOMETHING LIKE THAT? MAN, IF IT WASN'T FOR THOSE GLASSES..! AS IT IS, SHE AIN'T TOO BAD!

THE WAVES LAPPED UP THE SHORE AS IF IT WAS A FUDGE. I TOOK LUCY INTO MY ARMS AND SHE FITTED LIKE A KEY IN A LOCK! WE WERE ALONE. I LIKED THAT.

FINALLY, BABY! WE'RE ALONE. KISS ME, BABY! KISS ME HARD!

LET...ME...TAKE... OFF...MY...GLASSES..!

SHE PICKED THE GLASSES OFF HER FACE. HER LIPS SEARED INTO MINE AND I BRANDED MINE ON HERS. BUT I KNEW SOMETHING WAS WRONG...

MAN! HOW COULD JAMIE-BOY LEAVE YOU? WHAT A NUT!

LOOK INTO...MY... EYES, RUDY!

I LOOKED UP A SMILE ON MY FACE, THEN IT DISAPPEARED! LUCY HAD NO EYES. THEY WERE JUST TWO BIG SOCKETS WITH CANDLES INSIDE THEM. SOMEONE SCREAMED. IT WAS ME.

NOW YOU SEE WHY JAMIE-BOY LEFT ME!

EEEO-W!

SURGERY

The smooth marble floor of the sanitarium echoed with the steps of a tall man. The corridor funneled down into twin doors, over which was the sign: SURGERY. The man walked towards them, a slight twang of nervousness humming through his body. He knew, though, that it would disappear with thought . . . thought . . . and memory . . .

He remembered the cell, its walls padded with heavy material, its small, barred window allowing a spike of light to enter, its heavy iron door, which was just slammed shut: all this he remembered. Then, with a shiver, the man recalled his twin brother, Bob Laycoe, seated on the floor and mumbling to himself. Laycoe looked up.

"Well, Paul, did you expect," his voice cracked, "to find your brother in this sordid condition?"

"I'd like to talk to you, Bob," Paul Laycoe whispered, his voice as tender as possible. He tried to subdue the horrible fact that this wreck of a man, this beaten, broken remnant was once Robert Laycoe, the famous surgeon.

"Don't be so superior!" Bob screamed. "Say what you mean. You want to operate on my brain. That's it, isn't it?"

"Well, I . . . yes!" Paul said, a little ashamed.

"I won't allow it," Bob bellowed. "Do you hear? I won't allow you, a pipsqueak surgeon, to touch my brain with a knife!"

"The disease has to be cut out," Paul said quietly.

Bob had run into the shadows that were bunched in the corner of the room like a heavy cloak; but, even through them, his eyes gleamed. When he spoke, his voice seemed to come from blackness. "No, you're wrong. As soon as I get back into the swing of things, I'll be okay again. Let me perform one more operation . . . just one! That'll set me right!"

Paul winced with the suggestion. "You know that's impossible," he stated, peering into the glob of darkness that enveloped Bob.

Paul caught his breath. He was now on the fringe of the heavy blackness. He made out Bob's outline: the hunched shoulders, his head tucked in between them. Through the dense darkness that Paul now penetrated fully, he felt Bob's groping hands, clawing at him like talons.

He was horribly aware that Bob looked like something, something other than a man or a human being, looked like a mammoth bird, a gargantuan bird of prey. Paul screamed. Bob looked like a vulture and he was about to spring.

Even Bob's voice now assumed a squawk. "One more operation," it said. "One more!" That was all. Through the silent, black shadows, there came a guttural sound of held, choked breath.

The figure entered the swinging doors and saw the clean, white surgical room. Someone was on the operating table, etherized into unconsciousness. The figure donned a surgical mask and walked to the table. He leaned over it.

It spoke, its voice muffled through the mask. "Well, Paul," it said, "I told you all I needed was one more operation. Too bad no one could ever tell us apart. Heh?"

MONUMENTAL FEAT

THE FALL WINDS HIT HARD INTO CHAPPIE HALSTEAD'S CHEEKS, MAKING THEM TINGLE. HE FELT INVIGORATED AND ALIVE - AND HE LOOKED FORWARD WITH AN ALMOST TANGIBLE SENSE OF ANTICIPATION TO THE FOOTBALL GAME HIS FRIENDS INVITED HIM TO! THIS WAS THE FIRST ONE IN HIS LIFE HE WAS GOING TO SEE...

HEY, CHAPPIE—HOW'S IT *FEEL?* BET YOU CAN HARDLY WAIT TO GET TO THE FIELD?

GOT THAT OLD *ACNE* IN YOUR GUTS, EH? ME, TOO..!

YES... YES..!

DON, WHAT ARE THOSE... *MONUMENTS...* FOR?

MAN, DON'T YOU KNOW? YOU *REALLY* HAVEN'T BEEN *AROUND!* WHY, THE GREATS...THE *REAL GREATS*... ARE *BURIED* OUT THERE! THEY WERE SOMETHING!

CHAPPIE'S HEART SKIPPED A BEAT! HE COULDN'T TAKE HIS EYES OFF THE MONUMENTS, FEELING DRAWN TO THEM, FEELING A KINSHIP WITH THEM! EVEN AFTER THE GAME STARTED, HE STARED...

IN MEMORY OF CHOO CHOO CONROY

HE WAS OBLIVIOUS TO THE CHEERS... THE GROANS... THE HUSHED SILENCES THAT ACCOMPANIED TRICKY MANEUVERS! ALL HE SAW THAT DAY WERE THE MONUMENTS...

THE IMMORTALITY OF THE THREE GREATS BURIED THERE DUG INTO HIM LIKE THE PLAYERS' CLEATS INTO THE TURF...CHEWING HIM UP...TEARING HIS SOUL INTO LITTLE CHUNKS...

IN MEMORY OF BULL DOG DEVEY

AND...WHEN THE GAME WAS OVER...

HEY, CHAPPIE, WHAT'RE YOU SO QUIET ABOUT? DIDN'T YOU LIKE THE GAME?

HE DIDN'T EVEN SEE IT! HE KEPT ON STARING AT THE MONUMENTS...STARING AT 'EM...AND STARIN' AT 'EM!

BOY! I'D LOVE TO HAVE A MONUMENT... DEDICATED...TO ME!

EXIT →

THAT NIGHT...

I'VE GOT TO HAVE A MONUMENT— GOT TO HAVE MY NAME ON ONE... GOT TO BECOME A FOOTBALL GREAT...!

CHAPPIE THOUGHT...AND THOUGHT

WHEN THE NEXT DAY CAME, CHAPPIE BOUGHT A FOOTBALL, HIS FIRST ONE, CARESSING ITS PIGSKIN WITH TENDER FINGERS...

SP

IT WAS A WEEK DAY AND THERE WAS NO FOOTBALL AT THE BEAVER FIELD. A SILENCE...ALMOST LIKE A PALL...PERVADED THE STADIUM AS CHAPPIE ENTERED IT AND WALKED TO THE MONUMENTS, HIS NEW FOOTBALL FIRMLY GRIPPED IN HIS HANDS...AND THEY LOOKED LIKE TOMBSTONES IN THE BRISK, AUTUMN LONELINESS...

SOME DAY... MY NAME WILL BE ON A MONUMENT... RIGHT ALONG SIDE HERE...!

IN MEMORY OF

IN MEMORY OF

IN MEMORY

AND...HE MADE A VOW...

2

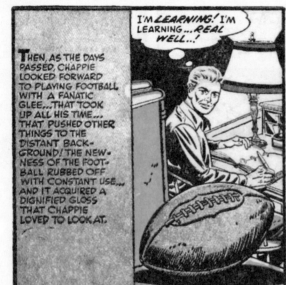

I'M *LEARNING!* I'M LEARNING...*REAL WELL...!*

THEN, AS THE DAYS PASSED, CHAPPIE LOOKED FORWARD TO PLAYING FOOTBALL WITH A FANATIC GLEE...THAT TOOK UP ALL HIS TIME... THAT PUSHED OTHER THINGS TO THE DISTANT BACK-GROUND! THE NEW-NESS OF THE FOOT-BALL RUBBED OFF WITH CONSTANT USE... AND IT ACQUIRED A DIGNIFIED GLOSS THAT CHAPPIE LOVED TO LOOK AT.

HE PRACTICED IN EVERY SPARE MOMENT...LEARNING PASSING...RUNNING...KICKING. HE SHARPENED HIS REFLEXES...STRENGTHENED HIS ANKLES...MADE HIS LEGS INTO LOCOMOTIVE GRANITE! HE PLAYED IN PICK-UP GAMES, WHERE HE EXCELLED. THEN, ONE DAY...

THAT'S IT, CHAPPIE!

THROUGHOUT THE WHOLE GAME, A SOLEMN-FACED MAN WATCHED CHAPPIE. THEN, AFTER IT WAS OVER, THE MAN AMBLED TO HIM AND SPOKE QUIETLY...WITH-OUT EMOTION... STATING PLAIN FACTS...FACTS THAT MADE CHAPPIE'S DREAM MORE REAL...NEARER... EVER NEARER...

I *LIKE* THE WAY YOU PLAY, CHAPPIE... LIKE IT *VERY MUCH!* HOW'D YOU LIKE TO *PLAY* FOR...THE *BEAVERS?* I'M ONE OF THEIR *SCOUTS!* NAME'S HYATT...LEM HYATT!

PLAY...FOR...THE ...BEAVERS?!! ARE YOU *KIDDING?* I'D *LOVE* IT! THIS... IS...THE...*DAY!*

SO, LATER, IN THE PRESENCE OF WITNESSES, CHAPPIE SIGNED A CONTRACT TO PLAY FOR THE BEAVERS...

GOOD BOY..!

...TO START ON ONE OF THE BEAVERS' FARM TEAMS...

LATER, CHAPPIE'S VOW WAS REPEATED...STRESSED... REITERATED...FOR THE SAKE OF THE DEAD!

I'M...COMING...(CHOKE)...!

IN MEMORY OF TIGER WALSH

3

So, later, Chappie had his first taste of professional football — and the taste was bitter. He swallowed it, though! He had to...

C'MON, GO...GO...!

He drove forward — driving, ever-driving — wanting to get to the top...impatient to get there...

..UGH..!

GET OFF YOUR FEET! C'MON, MOVE..!

Until, he was ready! He knew it... felt it...

GOOD...GOOD..!

YEA!

HURRAH!

CHAPPIE...

CHAPPIE...

HAWKS

Chappie Halstead's name got to be known — and its ring began to sound like greatness! He was climbing the ladder and the top was in sight! So, one day...

CHAPPIE, WE'RE BRINGING YOU UP!

YEAH! YOU'RE TOO GOOD TO STAY WITH THESE BUSH-LEAGUERS!

THE BEAVERS WANT YOU!

Later...

The goal was nearer, he could almost touch it!

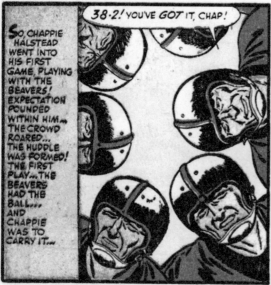

So, Chappie Halstead went into his first game, playing with the Beavers! Expectation pounded within him... The crowd roared... The huddle was formed! The first play... The Beavers had the ball... And Chappie was to carry it...

"38-2! You've GOT it, Chap!"

The line formed... The ball was snapped back to the quarterback... And on a quick-hand-off... Chappie found a hole in the line... And rammed through it...

He dodged one tackler... Stiff-armed another... Reversed his field... Changed again... Side-stepped a lunging man... And headed for the goal line! He covered five yards... Ten... Thirty... Fifty... Sixty... Heard the clomping cleats of the oppositions secondary behind him... And, suddenly, at the goal line... Was tackled...

He fell forward, the world spinning around him! There was the clear sight of the heavy goal-posts before him... He heard the thunk of his head banging up against them... Saw the haze... The blackness... The spinning, never-ending blackness...

This was the world of blankness... And blackness... For Chappie Halstead... The world without words... Without feeling... Without life!

"Lord! He's DEAD!"

"Boy! What a RUN he MADE! It was... GREAT!"

Everyone saw that Chappie had the touch of greatness... And that it had to be remembered! So, a vow made many long years ago...

...WAS FINALLY REALIZED!

IN MEMORY OF CHAPPIE HALSTEAD

IN MEMORY OF TIGER WALSH

THE END

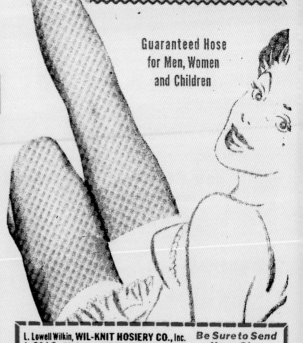

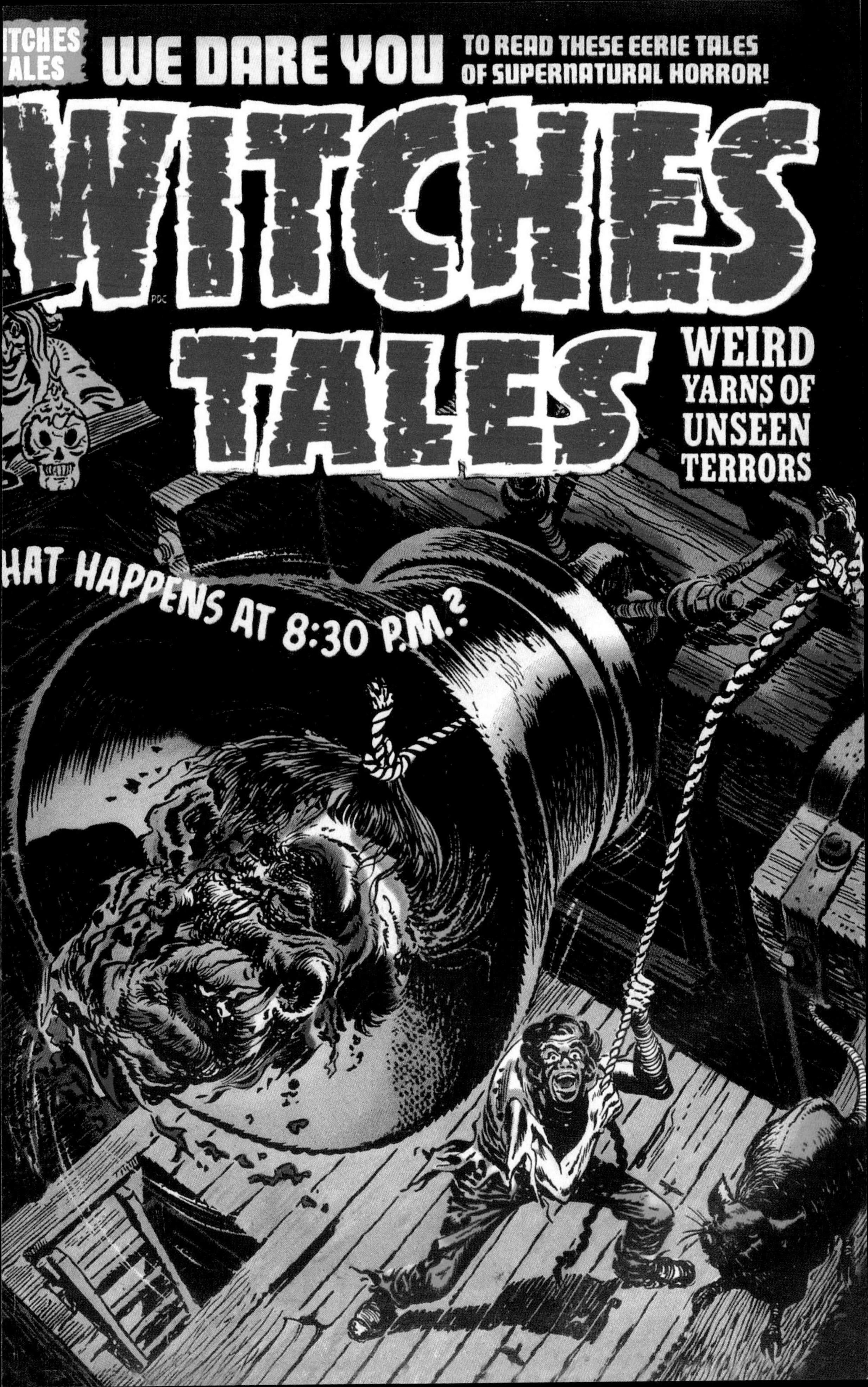
ITCHES
TALES
WE DARE YOU
TO READ THESE EERIE TALES
OF SUPERNATURAL HORROR!
WITCHES
TALES
WEIRD
YARNS OF
UNSEEN
TERRORS
HAT HAPPENS AT 8:30 P.M.?

WITCHES TALES, JUNE, 1954, VOL. 1, NO. 25, IS PUBLISHED BI-MONTHLY by WITCHES TALES, INC., 1860 Broadway, New York 23, N. Y. Entered as second class matter at the Post Office at New York, N. Y., under the Act of March, 3, 1879. Single copies, 10c. Subscription rates, 10 issues for $1.00 in the U. S. and possessions, elsewhere $1.50. All names in this periodical are entirely fictitious and no identification with actual persons is intended. Contents copyrighted, 1954, by Witches Tales, Inc., New York, City. Printed in the U.S.A. Title registered in U. S. Patent Office.

WELCOME

WE WANT YOUR LETTERS! All kinds... big ones, fat ones, skinny ones, all sizes and shapes! And... what do we want you to write about?

We want your opinion on that new, terrific, four-power horror pact that CHAMBER OF CHILLS, TOMB OF TERROR, BLACK CAT MYSTERY and WITCHES TALES have entered into... sort of a blood pool! How do you rate this shock king's domain?

Tell us what you like about these four distinctive books that now come to you during a two-month period, a mag appearing on your newsstands every two weeks.

What is the impact of BLACK CAT MYSTERY, where man meets man in a mad clash of reality? How different is the design of WITCHES TALES, the mag that chills your spine and tickles your funny bone? How far are you sent by TOMB OF TERROR, whose stories are ripped from the many unexplored voids? How deep are you in the incredible sphere of the supernatural, which CHAMBER OF CHILLS takes you to?

We want the answers to these questions in your letters. Don't choke up... let us have it, both barrels. All you do is, write to:
WITCHES TALES, INC.
1860 Broadway
New York 23, N. Y.

WITCHES TALES

CONTENTS NO. 25

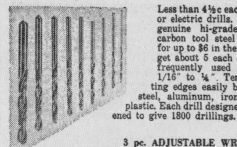

THE TICKET

YOU'RE A *GUNMAN*, LOLLO GIBRIDA. YOU'RE FAST WITH THE TRIGGER...AND YOU'RE *WANTED* BY THE *LONDON POLICE*. YES, LOLLO, YOU'RE BEING CHASED...

TWEEEET

YOU'VE JUMPED THE FENCE, LOLLO...BUT WHERE TO NOW? IT'S NIGHT AND A ROTTEN CHILL BITES INTO YOU LIKE A SNAKE. FOG'S ALL AROUND, YOU FEEL *TRAPPED* AND YOU *CAN'T SEE*...

WH...WHERE AM I? CAN'T... (GASP)...RUN ANY MORE!

SUDDENLY, YOU HEAR IT... *TWO* DRAWN-OUT SOUNDS, LIKE HORRENDOUS *MOANS* OF A DEAD *GIANT.* YOU FREEZE, LOLLO... AND *HOPE...*

FTOOOM
FTOOOM

THEN YOU SEE IT... THE THIN LINE OF A BOW OF A SHIP CUTTING THE FOG. IT'S *BLACK* AND *SHARP...* AND YOU'RE A PEBBLE NEXT TO THIS ROCK OF THE SEA...

F-FOG HORNS! A... *SHIP!* LOOK AT THE SIZE OF IT!

IT'S GIGANTIC, ALL RIGHT, LOLLO. YOU STARE AT IT. THEN, YOU GET AN IDEA...

A SHIP! PROBABLY *GOING OUT* OF THE *COUNTRY!* JUST SITTING THERE ... WAITING FOR *ME* TO *BUY A TICKET!* HEH-HEH! THAT'S ALL I GOT TO DO... JUST BUY A *TICKET...!*

YOU'RE SATISFIED WITH THE IDEA, LOLLO, WHY NOT *SLEEP* ON IT? SO YOU *CRAWL* INTO A NICE, DARK CORNER... NOT SO COZY BECAUSE IT *SMELLS* OF BRINE AND SWEAT... BUT IT'LL DO TILL THE MORNING...

MORNING COMES, FOG STILL AROUND, BUT NOW IT'S ADVANTAGEOUS, HARD TO RECOGNIZE YOU IN IT. SLOWLY, YOU MEANDER TO THE TICKET AGENCY. YOU'RE *SATISFIED...*

MAN, THIS IS A CINCH!

YOU ENTER. A FEW *PEOPLE* ARE *AHEAD* OF YOU, BUT YOU *WAIT* YOUR TURN LIKE A GOOD *CITIZEN.* BUT YOU LOOK AROUND, JUST TO MAKE SURE THERE ARE *NO BOBBIES...*

NOBODY! SO FAR, SO GOOD...

THE *MAN* IN *FRONT* OF YOU BUYS *HIS* TICKET, NOW YOU PUT YOUR MONEY DOWN ON THE TILL, BUT IT'S *NO GOOD,* LOLLO. SHOCK RUNS THROUGH YOU, LOLLO, BECAUSE...

OH, I'M TERRIBLY SORRY, SIR! THERE ARE *NO MORE TICKETS AVAILABLE.* THE LAST *ONE* WAS *SOLD* TO THAT *GENTLEMAN* BEFORE YOU. SORRY...

WHAT!

BUT IT'S NOT OVER FOR YOU, LOLLO, THE GUY IN FRONT OF YOU HAS THAT TICKET, YOU *FOLLOW HIM...* FOR A *REASON...*

GOT TO GET IT *AWAY* FROM HIM...BUT *AT NIGHT...* AT NIGHT!

Ye Shop

YES, AT *NIGHT*, LOLLO...WHEN YOU DO YOUR BEST WORK, YOU'LL *WAIT...* WHILE HE HAS A MEAL WITH A YOUNG LADY...

LOOK AT THAT! WHAT A LAUGH!

YOU'LL *WAIT* FOR HIM, LOLLO, YOU'LL EAT YOUR HEART OUT WHILE HE'S WITH HER IN HER APARTMENT, BUT, IT'S *NIGHT*, LOLLO... IT'S NIGHT...

OLD... GEEZER...

THEN THE *WAITING* IS *OVER.* HE COMES OUT, YOU *HIDE* IN THE SHADOWS...

THEN YOU *SPRING.* YOU *GRAB HIM* FROM BEHIND, YOUR GLOVED HAND AROUND HIS NOSE... *SHUTTING OFF* HIS *AIR...*

MMMF

NOW... FOR THAT... TICKET...

YOU THROW HIM TO THE GROUND, YOU'VE *GOT* HIM, LOLLO... GOT HIM *GOOD...*

I NEED THAT *TICKET...*

MMMFFFFFF

HE DIES, LOLLO...QUIETLY AND EFFICIENTLY. HE'S STIFF ON THE GROUND, OFFERING NO RESISTANCE AS YOU *GO THROUGH* HIS *WALLET.* HE DOESN'T EVEN SMILE WHEN YOU DO...AS YOU *FIND* WHAT YOU *WANT...*

HEH! HEH! HERE...IT... IS...!

3

YOU'RE *SATISFIED*, LOLLO, YOU PUT THE *TICKET* INSIDE YOUR COAT POCKET AND TURN FOR THE SHIP AS YOU *WALK*, THOUGH, A *SQUARE PIECE* OF *PAPER FLUTTERS* TO THE GROUND, *UNSEEN* BY YOU...

IT'S THE *TICKET*, LOLLO...

SORRY, SIR...BUT I'LL HAVE TO SEE YOUR PASSENGER TICKET. I CANNOT ALLOW YOU ABOARD WITHOUT IT!

BUT, I TELL YOU, I'VE LOST IT!

YOU TURN AROUND, KNOWING IT'S THE ONLY WAY...

IF YOU CAN *FIND* IT..?

YEAH, YEAH....I KNOW..!

YOU SLOWLY *RETRACE* EVERY *STEP* YOU TOOK THAT LED TO THE *SHIP*...LOOKING, SEARCHING FOR THAT *TICKET* TO FREEDOM. SUDDENLY, YOU SCREAM MUTELY...

NO...

THERE, NOT MORE THAN TEN FEET IN FRONT OF YOU, IS A HUGE *HULK* OF A *MAN*...BENDING DOWN...*STOOPING* OVER TO PICK UP A SQUARE *PIECE* OF *PAPER*...

TH--THAT GUY! HE'S FOUND THE TICKET...

IT'S THE ONLY WAY, LOLLO, YOU'VE GOT TO ASK HIM FOR IT. POLITELY, YOU WALK TO HIM, LOOK UP INTO HIS TOUGH FACE, AND SAY IT AS NICELY AS POSSIBLE...

CAN I... *HAVE THAT?* IT--IT'S *MINE!*

YEAH?!! *PROVE IT!* WHAT'S YOUR *NAME?*

NAME! WHOSE NAME? OF COURSE... THE *MAN* YOU *KILLED.* BUT YOU DON'T KNOW IT. YOU DIDN'T TAKE THE TIME TO FIND OUT WHAT IT WAS, YOU'RE TRAPPED...AND YOU'VE GOT TO *FIGHT* YOUR WAY OUT. YOU *SWING* HITTING THE GUY IN THE *PIT* OF HIS *STOMACH*...

GIVE... IT...TO... ME!

OOF...

4

THE GUY IS *STRONG*, THOUGH. HE GETS YOU, LOLLO...GETS YOU IN A *DEATH GRIP*...CRUSHING YOU TO HIM... SQUEEZING THE *AIR* OUT OF YOU...CRUNCHING YOUR *RIBS*...

WISE GUY HUH?

UNN..! UNN..H..H

YOU *CAN'T WRIGGLE* OUT OF IT. THE GRIP IS *TOO TIGHT...TOO STRONG*. YOU FEEL EVERY OUNCE OF *STRENGTH PUSHED* OUT OF YOU. DEATH COMES IN SHORT GASPS. IT'S *ALMOST* THE *END*, LOLLO. BUT YOU USE YOUR *THUMBS*, AIMING FOR HIS EYES...

WANT TO PLAY, RUNT? SO PLAY...

AND YOU STRIKE...

YAAAHHH!

AND YOU LET LOOSE WITH ALL THE *STRENGTH* YOU HAVE LEFT...

YOU *PICK* UP THE *TICKET*. YOU ALMOST *LOST* YOUR *LIFE* FOR IT. YOU FEEL GROGGY, LOLLO, AS YOU *SHUFFLE BACK* TO THE *SHIP*. YOUR HAND GRIPS THE TICKET, NEVER WANTING TO LET IT GO...

YOU HAND IT TO THE SURPRISED OFFICER, WHO WATCHES YOU *SNICKER* UNDER YOUR BREATH. HE'S PERPLEXED, LOLLO. WHY NOT? HE DOESN'T *KNOW* WHAT YOU *WENT THROUGH* TO GET THAT *TICKET*...

HEH... HEH...!

YOU'RE ABOARD, LOLLO GIBRIDA. THE *SHIP* MOVES OUT AND YOU *LAUGH HYSTERICALLY*. YOU STAND ON THE STERN, LAUGHING, NEVER BOTHERING TO FIND OUT THE *NAME OF THE SHIP* YOU'RE ON...

TITANIC

THE END

5

Mother Mongoose's NURSERY CRIMES

A DILLAR, A DOLLAR, A TEN O'CLOCK SCHOLAR!

THE TEACHER SANG A FIERY TUNE!

BUT IT WAS THE SCHOLAR WHO HAD THE LESSON TO TEACH—

AND NOW HE COMES IN AT NOON!

Mother Mongoose's NURSERY CRIMES

RITA RIPER RIPPED A WRECK OF ROTTEN ROSES.

A WRECK OF ROTTEN ROSES RITA RIPER RIPPED?

YES, RITA RIPER RIPPED A WRECK OF ROTTEN ROSES---

'CAUSE HERE'S THE WRECK OF ROTTEN ROSES RITA RIPER RIPPED!

WHAT'S IN A NAME?

The editor was balling out Tom Powers once again.

"Listen, Tom," he shouted. "If you're going to write stories about ghouls and vampires and such, at least give them proper names. Sam, the vampire; Sadie, the witch; Gregory, the ghoul; Morris, the mummy! What kind of stuff are you giving me?"

Tom Powers smiled. "Listen, Gordon," he said. "Don't those names give a touch of realism to the stories? Doesn't Morris, the mummy, sound better than Garffo, the mummy? Don't you think it's more probable to meet a vampire named Samuel than one called Krako?"

"Don't you hand me any of that tommy-rot!" said Gordon. "If you want to deal with the stupid supernatural, go ahead and do it. If it's a good story, I'll buy it. But you give your creatures names that would fit. Yes, Krako, Garffo, Ygor, Barto may sound silly to your half-baked brain, but those are the names I want!"

"Listen, pal," said Tom Powers, trying to calm the editor. "There's no reason to get excited."

"But I've gone over this with you a hundred times!"

"I know. Easy, take it easy. Let me explain a misconception to you. Don't you understand why people expect supernatural creatures to have those crazy names of yours?"

"I'm not asking for a lecture," protested the editor.

"Just let me finish, Gordon. Those names were used because most of those supernatural stories grew up in foreign countries. So foreign or pseudo-foreign names seem natural for the characters."

"So I have no objections," said Gordon.

"But you should have!" said Tom Powers. "Don't you see what I'm trying to do? I'm trying to give supernatural stories an American flavor. I want people to think it could happen here. So you've got to give the people in your supernatural stories popular names!"

Gordon couldn't take any more. "Get out of here," he told Tom Powers. "And don't come back till every one of your monsters have the right names. Leave American names to the historians! We deal in fiction, and the fictional supernatural creature is a foreigner!"

Tom Powers didn't wait for another word. Bread and butter was more important to him than any whim. He tipped his hat, said good-bye, and told Gordon he'd be back with the most foreign names ever made.

The editor smiled when Tom Powers had exited. "Got to give the guy credit," he said. "He's sure got spunk."

"Who's got spunk?" said a voice.

"Huh?" Gordon swung round in his chair to face two ghoulish figures in vampire-like capes.

"Who are you?" the editor said in a startled voice.

"Just a couple of vampires," answered one of them. "My name's Thomas. My partner's name is Eddie. And you've got a case, boy."

The last words Gordon heard as teeth dug into his neck were: "You traitor, you!"

ALI BARBER AND THE FORTY THIEVES

ALI BARBER WAS PROUD OF TWO THINGS-- HIS MASTERY WITH THE SCISSORS, AND HIS FIERCE PRIDE. BUT ALI BARBER COULDN'T ADMIT EVEN TO HIMSELF THAT HE WAS A TERRIBLE BARBER! HE JUST *WOULDN'T!*

I'LL BREAK THESE CRUMMY RAZORS! I'LL SMASH THEM AND GET MYSELF SOME REAL KITS! THEY'RE NO GOOD! THEY'RE RUINING ME!

SMASH!

WHY... CAN'T I... EVER GET A COMPLIMENT? *JUST ONE!* THAT'S ALL I ASK... WHAT'S WRONG WITH ME? I KNOW I'M GOOD! *I KNOW IT!*

SO ALI WENT HOME TO HIS MODEST LITTLE HOME WHERE HIS CHARMING LITTLE WIFE WAITED FOR HIM-- WHAT WAS HE GOING TO DO? HOW WAS HE GOING TO TELL WHAT HAD HAPPENED?

'LO, SWEETHEART DARLING-- I NEED SOME MONEY FOR A NEW HAT. AND SINCE YOU'VE BEEN WORKING OVERTIME, I THOUGHT--

THOUGHT--?

YOU--*THOUGHT!* ALWAYS NAGGING AT ME! YOU WANT THIS! YOU WANT THAT! STOP IT! I'M *TIRED* OF IT! YOU CAN'T HAVE IT! I DON'T HAVE THE MONEY! *UNDERSTAND? NO MONEY!*

BAM

DARLING, DID EVERYTHING GO ALL RIGHT WITH YOUR BUSINESS? I MEAN-- NOTHING *WRONG*... DID IT?

I LOST THREE MORE CUSTOMERS TODAY, MAY... I MADE-- FOUR DOLLARS AND SOME CHANGE. FOUR DOLLARS AFTER FOURTEEN HOURS OF WAITING...

ALI--MAYBE YOU... YOU OUGHT TO GIVE UP YOUR STORE! YOU COULD GO INTO INSURANCE-- OR MY BROTHER HORACE COULD FIX YOU UP WITH A CLERICAL--

NO! I'M AN *ARTIST!* YOU DON'T UNDER- STAND! *NO ONE UNDERSTANDS!* I'M THE BEST BARBER IN THE WORLD! LOOK AT THESE RAZORS!

MADE IN GERMANY! MADE IN SWITZERLAND! MADE IN ITALY AND BRITAIN AND THE UNITED STATES! THE BEST THAT MONEY CAN BUY! AND NOW I'LL *USE* THEM! I'LL MAKE A *NAME* FOR MYSELF!

SO ALI TRIED AGAIN. HE CURBED HIS TEMPER. HE BOUGHT NOTHING BUT THE FINEST BLADES, THE BEST LOTIONS, THE MOST EXPENSIVE OF ALL HAIR TONICS, AND ALI *TRIED!*

I SAID CAREFUL WITH THE BACK, YOU! I WANT A TRIM NEAR THE EARS! REMEMBER THAT!

YES, SIR...YOU'LL BE CUT WELL, I PROMISE YOU!

... AND TRIED...

DO YOU CALL THAT A HAIRCUT? DO A LITTLE BETTER ON THE SHAVE, WILL YA? EASY NOW-- EASY! YOU'RE SCRAPING ME!

YES SIR...JUST HOLD STILL NOW.., PLEASE, SIR...

... AND TRIED...

OWWW! THAT'S THE THIRD TIME YOU'VE CUT ME! THAT'S ENOUGH!

PLEASE, MISTER... LET ME FINISH YOUR HAIR! *PLEASE!*

BUT PEOPLE JUST DIDN'T SEEM TO LIKE HIS WORK. ALI REDUCED HIS RATES. THAT HELPED A BIT. ALI GAVE AWAY FREE GIFT COUPONS. THAT HELPED EVEN MORE. ALI PROMISED ONE FREE SHAVE TO A CUSTOMER ON SATURDAYS. THAT HELPED TREMENDOUSLY. BUT NOTHING HELPED...

TERRIBLE! I WOULDN'T COME IN HERE AGAIN IF YOU GAVE AWAY *TEN* FREE SHAVES!

WAIT-- PLEASE!

DROP DEAD! NUTS TO YOU!

PLEASE--! GIVE ME ANOTHER CHANCE!

NOT ON YOUR LIFE!

AND HIS TROUBLES INCREASED! TOOLS HAD TO BE PAID FOR. OVERHEAD HAD TO BE BALANCED. RENT HAD TO BE RECKONED WITH.. UNTIL ONE NIGHT WHEN ALI THOUGHT HIS WORRIES COULDN'T POSSIBLY BE MUCH WORSE...

WHEN DO I GET MY BILLS PAID? YOU'RE TWO MONTHS BEHIND IN YOUR RENT!

IF YOU'LL ONLY GIVE ME ANOTHER TWO--

LISTEN, BARBER...I'LL GIVE YOU JUST TWO DAYS TO PAY UP OR GET OUT!

Y-YES...

SO ALI WAS UP AGAINST THE WALL. AND WHAT MADE IT EVEN MORE GALLING WAS THAT OF ALL THE NEIGHBORS ON HIS BLOCK, ALI BARBER WAS THE POOREST, MOST MISERABLE FAILURE OF THEM ALL!

ALL OF THEM ARE MAKING OUT! ALL OF THEM BUT *ME*! SOMETHING HAS TO BE DONE! THEY CAN'T KEEP ME DOWN! I *KNOW* I'LL BE FAMOUS. I JUST *KNOW* IT! I'LL PROVE IT!

BUT ALI WAS AT THE END OF HIS ROPE. HE TOSSED AND TURNED IN HIS SLEEP! HE MOANED AND GROANED AND WAILED WHEN OTHERS COULDN'T HEAR HIM. HE TRIED TO THINK OF A WAY OUT -- *ANY* WAY OUT. AND THAT NEXT MORNING, AS HE CAME TO OPEN HIS SHOP...

NO MORE CUSTOMERS! HOW AM I GOING TO BUILD UP MY TRADE? HOW AM I GOING TO PAY MY BILLS, AND BUY MY WIFE A NEW HAT, AND BE FAMOUS? HOW AM I-- WAIT! I'VE GOT IT!

WHY NOT GO TO THESE FELLOWS DIRECTLY? SURE-- IT'S A FORMAL DINNER. THEY *HAVE* TO BE SHAVED, DON'T THEY? AND IF I WORK FAST, I'LL MAKE A MINT. WHY NOT?

BUSINESSMAN'S DINNER
BLUE ROOM - 4 P.M.
FORMAL

SO ALI LOOKED AT THE REGISTER, FOUND FORTY NAMES SIGNED THERE AS BUSINESSMEN, GATHERED ALL HIS SHAVING KITS TOGETHER, AND MINUTES LATER, FACED THE DOOR OF HIS FIRST PROSPECT...

FORTY BUSINESSMEN AT A DOLLAR A HEAD WILL GIVE ME FORTY DOLLARS -- I'LL HAVE ENOUGH FOR---

REMEMBER--- WE'RE ALL BUSINESSMEN, SEE? WE'RE MEETIN' TO DISCUSS BUSINESS!

HA, HA... SOME BUSINESS! HOW WE'RE GONNA BUMP OFF RIVAL MOBS!

SHADDUP, LOU! NOW EVERYONE GO TO YOUR ROOMS! IF THE BULLS EVER GET WISE THAT THE FORTY MOST WANTED CRIMINALS ARE HERE UNDER ONE ROOF, THEY'LL HAVE A FIELD DAY. WE GOTTA BE CAREFUL! *VERY CAREFUL!* THE MINUTE SOMEONE GETS SUSPICIOUS, WE *BLOW!* UNDERSTAND?

GOOD LORD--!

I WON'T TELL ANYONE! I'LL JUST COLLECT MY REWARD WITHOUT A FUSS. DEAD OR ALIVE... THERE'S A PRICE ON EACH OF THEIR HEADS! *DEAD OR ALIVE!*

ALI RAN BACK TO HIS SHOP. HE PILED RAZORS, STACKED SCISSORS, TIED TOGETHER SHARPENED BLADES--ALL INTO A HUGE BOX. ALI'S HEART WAS SINGING WITH JOY! HE WAS HAPPY! HE WAS GOING TO BE *FAMOUS!*

THEY'LL ALL BE IN THEIR ROOMS--ONE BY ONE--ALONE! HA, HA--I'LL SHOW MY NEIGHBORS, I'LL SHOW THAT LANDLORD, THOSE OTHERS--THAT I'M *GOOD!*

HOTEL BARBER, SIR... THE HOTEL PROVIDES *FREE* SHAVES FOR EACH MALE CUSTOMER, SIR!

FORTY DOORS WERE GLADLY OPENED. ALI BARBER WAS ALWAYS GREETED WITH A WARM, WELCOME SMILE...

MY PLEASURE, MISTER! MY PLEASURE!

FORTY TIMES ALI BARBER CLOSED A DOOR BEHIND HIM, THE MEN WE HAPPY TO GET THEIR SHAVES...

BE RIGHT WITH YOU!

THESE HOODS THINK OF EVERYTHING!

AND FORTY TIMES, ALI BARBER LEFT LAUGHING...*THEIR* HEADS OFF!

HAH! I'M *HEADING* FOR RICHES!

YAAARRGURGH!

LATER...

FINISHED! FORTY HEADS WITHOUT CHANGING THE BLADE! NOW TO COLLECT THE REWARD! GADS! BUT THOSE HOODS WERE SHREWD...HAVING THEIR OWN POLICE UNIFORMS! WELL, BETTER TELL THE MANAGER TO CHANGE THAT SIGN! HEH!

BUT THE SIGN *HAD* BEEN CHANGED...CHANGED SOMETIME BEFORE ALI BARBER HAD GONE TO WORK!

OH, NO! THEY *WERE* COPS!

ACTIVITIES
BUSINESSMAN'S DINNER
CANCELLED
TONIGHT----9 P.M.
ANNUAL POLICE SERGEANT'S
Forum

THE END

LOOK HERE! for BIG MONEY MAKING OPPORTUNITIES for MONEY-SAVING OFFERS and SERVICES

START OR ADD TO YOUR COLLECTION WITH

FREE 100 Exciting BRITISH EMPIRE STAMPS!

to Make New Friends!

He walked down the infested street, a smile on his face. Serenely, a rat sat on a garbage can, watching him. He erased the smile. Something now bothered him...

HMM. PLACE DESERTED. NOBODY AROUND. WONDER WHAT'S UP?

SHLEP SHLUP SHLEP SHLUP SHLEP SHLUP...

Coming further, he became disturbed. He tilted his battered hat back to the peak of his head, allowing two antennae to pop out...

NOT A SOUL AROUND. KIND OF... UH...CREEPY. WHERE COULD EVERYBODY HAVE GONE?

EVEN AS HE ROUNDED A CORNER, FACING A DILAPIDATED STREET, THERE WAS A STILLNESS AND AN EMPTINESS THAT DISTURBED HIM. SUDDENLY, A SHAFT OF LIGHT PEEKED DOWN. A YOUNG BOY WAS LOOKING OUT, TOWARDS HIM...

HEY!

QUICKLY, AS IF TERROR WERE GOADING HER, THE BOY'S MOTHER PULLED HIM AWAY...

TOMMY! WHAT'S THE MATTER WITH YOU? DON'T STAY THERE!

TWO SHUTTERS SLAMMED, KNIFING THE SHAFT OF LIGHT INTO DARKNESS...

WHAT GIVES HERE?

SLAM!

PERPLEXED, AGITATED BY THE EMPTINESS THAT HUNG LIKE A SHROUD OVER EVERY STREET HE WALKED UPON, THE MAN SEEMED TO WANDER AIMLESSLY, A' BELFRY CLOCK SOMEWHERE TOLLED EIGHT TIMES...

BONG BONG BONG BONG BONG BONG BONG BONG

SHLEP SHLEP SHLEP SHLEP SHLEP

THEN HE STOPPED, A CREASE OF A SMILE EASING INTO HIS FACE. A SHORT DISTANCE AWAY WAS A MAN, WARMING HIMSELF BY A BRIGHT, ORANGE FIRE...

WELL, HALLELUJAH! A PERSON!

HE DIDN'T KNOW WHY HE SHUFFLED SILENTLY TO THE FIRE. IT JUST SEEMED TO FIT THE VILLAGE'S FOREBODING TONE. SLOWLY, HE TAPPED THE MAN ON THE SHOULDER. THE MAN TURNED AROUND, THE LOOK OF FEAR ON HIS FACE...

UM, EXCUSE ME.

TAP TAP

YAAA-III!

HE EXPLAINED, WANTING TO KNOW WHERE EVERYBODY WAS. THE STRANGER EASED UP A LITTLE, STILL SLIGHTLY CAUTIOUS. HE WAS INVITED TO SIT DOWN. THE FIRE'S GLOW WAS WARM...

SURE, IT'S LONELY, BUSTER! YOU BETTER SIT DOWN. DON'T YOU KNOW WHAT'S HAPPENING AT 8:30 PM?!

THANKS... WHAT DO YOU MEAN...8:30?!! WHAT'S GOING ON? WHAT'S HAPPENING?!!

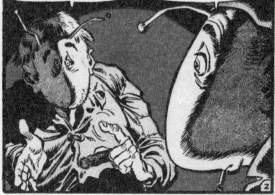

HE FELT THE STRANGER'S COMFORTING ARM AROUND HIS SHOULDER...

NOW, NO NEED TO GET EXCITED! BUT,...WELL...UH... I THINK YOU'D BETTER CLEAR OUT,...AS BEST YOU CAN! IT'S GOING TO BE PRETTY ROUGH AROUND HERE!

ROUGH ?!! THEN... WHY DON'T WE BOTH GO ? WHAT ARE YOU STAYING FOR ?

THE MAN SAW THE STRANGER'S FACE SLOWLY TURN TOWARDS THE FIRE, ITS BEADY EYES AND PURSED MOUTH NOW IN A MASK OF GRIMNESS...

ME ? I'M TIRED OF RUNNING, I'VE HAD ENOUGH OF IT! IT'LL CATCH UP... SOONER OR LATER, HOW LONG CAN A GUY... RUN!

HE SAW THE STRANGER'S LOOK... IMPLORING, URGING...

YOU BETTER GO! RUN, MISTER! DO... ANYTHING! JUST GET OUT OF HERE!

Y-YEA, YEAH! S-SO LONG! I'LL SEE YOU... GULP... I GUESS!

HE GOT UP...AND SHUFFLED OFF INTO THE DARKNESS. HE FELT IT, THOUGH... A PANG OF FEAR THAT DUG INTO HIM LIKE A DAGGER. HE COULDN'T HELP BUT LOOK BACK OVER HIS SHOULDER AT THE BROKEN, WEAKENED STRANGER...

SHLEP SHLUP SHLEP

OVER HIS HEAD, THE STEEPLE CLOCK READ...

SHLEP SHLUP

A SHIVER WIGGLED UP HIS SPINE. OUT OF THE CORNER OF HIS EYE, BY A RUN-DOWN FENCE, WEEDY AND OOZY, HE SAW A SHADOW THAT WAS AMORPHOUS, INTANGIBLE...

SHLEP SHLUP

THE SHADOW TURNED INTO A MAN, WHOSE BONY HANDS GRIPPED THE TOP OF THE FENCE. THE MAN LEAPED OVER IT...

THE GUY WAS RUNNING. HE WAS SURE OF IT. SUDDENLY, HE FELT A SCURRYING BEHIND HIM AND THE TRAMPLE OF FEET MOVING RAPIDLY... HE WHIRLED...

SOMETHING WAS HAPPENING. IT WAS LIKE A SNOW-BALL ON A HILL, ROLLING DOWNWARD AND GETTING BIGGER. SOMEBODY ELSE BRUSHED BY HIM... AND RAN OFF...

HE PUT HIS GRIMY FINGERNAILS TO HIS MOUTH. SWEAT BEADS FORMED ON HIS INKY BROW. FEAR... COLD AND ABSOLUTE ... CHOKED HIM, KNOTTING HIS THROAT IN AN UNCONSUMING BALL...

LORD... LORD....!

AND... HE BEGAN TO RUN...

SHLEP SHLUP SHLEP SHLUP SHLEP SHLUP

SHLEP SHLUP

SHLUF SHLEP SHLUP

BUT... HE DIDN'T KNOW WHERE TO GO. EVERY AVENUE SEEMED BLOCKED, EVERY DIRECTION SEEMED TO END IN A MAZE. HE HEADED FOR AN ALLEY, TRIPPING OVER AN ASH-CAN. THE METALLIC DIN RESOUNDED IN CLAMOR...

CRASSHH!

SHLEP SHLUP SHLEP SHLUP SHLEP SHLUP SHLEP SHLUP

HE VEERED, SLUSHING AWAY FROM A RED GLASS EYE, AND RAN WITH INCREASED FERVOR. HE CHURNED THE GROUND BENEATH HIM IN HUGE GLOBS OF WETTNESS, HEADING INTO DARKNESS AND BLIND DIRECTION...

DEAD END

UNTIL HE FACED AN EMPTY FETID STREET. HE STOOD ALONE... HORRIBLY ALONE... IN THE MUCK THAT HAD THE SWEET SCENT OF HOME...

WH-WHERE CAN I GO? WHY AM I RUNNING? WHAT THE BLAZES IS GOING ON, ANY HOW?

4

HIS MIND DANCED WITH CRAZINESS. HE WAS CAUGHT, HYSTERICALLY CAUGHT BY A DEATH HE KNEW WAS COMING. DAZED, UNBELIEVING, HE BACKED UP AGAINST A STORE WINDOW, TRYING TO GET HIS BEARINGS, TO SET THINGS RIGHT...

GOT TO THINK...! IT'S GOING T HAPPEN...AT...8:30! WH-Wh TIME IS IT...NOW?

THE STORE'S INTERIOR WAS LIT BY A SINGLE BULB. HE LOOKED INSIDE, NOTICING THE CLOCK HANGING ON THE WALL. HE GULPED, THEN SCREAMED...

YEOW!

THE UGLY MYSTERY, BLACK AND IMPENDING, BEGAN TO CLOSE IN. HIS BLOOD POUNDED FURIOUSLY. IT WAS ALL SO HORRIFYING THAT A WHITE DROP THAT SPLATTERED ON HIS SHOULDER SEEMED UNCOMMON...SEEMED OUT-OF-PLACE...

EH? WHA--? RAIN?!!

IT WASN'T RAIN THOUGH! THE DROPS WEREN'T COOLING! THEY WERE HOT, COMING DOWN IN A STEADY STREAM... SEARING EVERYTHING AROUND HIM IN WHITE-HEAT...

NO, NO! NOT RAIN...

THE STREAM POURED DOWN IN ENDLESS, SEARING PATTERNS...SEARING EVERYTHING...SCORCHING THE STREET. HE SMELLED HIS OWN FLESH...IN ITS SCORCHING, ROTTED MIASMA...AND HE REALIZED WHAT WAS HAPPENING...AND WHAT HE WAS...

I KNOW...I KNOW! IT'S...8:30...

HE WAS A GERM!

THE STREAM...NOW STREAKS...BEGAN TO BURN HIM... BURN HIM ALIVE...

EIGHT...THIRTY... EIGHT...THIR... YEOOWWWW!

AND THE STREAKS WERE...ALL-CONSUMING...ALL POWERFUL...X-RAYS!

THE END.

Mother Mongoose's NURSERY CRIMES

HICKORY DICKORY DOCK TRIED TO STEAL THE CLOCK...

TICK TICK TICK TICK TICK TICK

AT A QUARTER TO FOUR, HE GOT TO THE DOOR

TICK-SQUEERP TICK-SQUEERP

BUT THE DOOR HAD BEEN JUICED, AND THE SPRINGS BROKE LOOSE!

TICK-WHOOOMP!

NOT THE CLOCK'S... BUT HICKORY DICKORY DOCK'S!

Mother Mongoose's NURSERY CRIMES

LITTLE JACK HORNER SAT IN A CORNER

EATING A STRANGE LOOKING PIE.

BUT HE WASN'T WELL-FED TILL HE PULLED OUT THAT HEAD...

AND SAID:

WHAT A GHOUL BOY AM I!

LOVE PROBLEM

The man and woman could only live and love by moonlight. Night was their day, and day their night. Yet they never minded it. This was natural to vampires.

But Cecelia and Gregory had another problem, a problem that could destroy their love.

That problem was expressed clearly one clear and beautiful night as they walked together near the marshes.

"Gregory," Cecelia said. "You must get money somewhere. We can't go on this way any longer."

Gregory looked at her, and said, "Darling, I know you're right. And believe me, I do want to marry you. But I just can't seem to make ends meet. And I surely don't want you to live in any old tomb. You've got to have the best."

He kissed her then, a cold and wonderful kiss that chilled her with a vampire passion.

"Be patient," he said. "It won't be too much longer."

But the weeks flew by, and there was no change. Gregory couldn't hold a job. They all ended up in the same way as that night watchman stint. He couldn't control his great lust for blood, and instead of staying on the job, he travelled the city seeking a snack here, a snack there. It was obvious they had to fire him.

So this time Cecelia had to give an ultimatum. She realized she wasn't getting any younger.

"Gregory," she told him one black night. "It hurts to say this; but I must. I can't wait any longer for you. You must get enough money to marry me or we will have to part."

The words hurt Gregory even more. But he knew she was right. "I will make one last effort," he promised. "You will see that our love will not fail."

The next night, Gregory put his efforts to work. He got a job in a bakery rolling rolls and baking cake. The salary wasn't bad, and it looked as if it could build into something big.

He promised Cecelia he would control his desire for blood, curbing it to weekends. And Cecelia was thrilled. She was sure that he had at last found his niche in society.

She was right, but not as right as she expected to be. He had found his niche in society, all right, Lenore Society, the baker's daughter! And Lenore didn't care if he worked or not. Her father's bakery was doing a rolling business.

So that was the way the love problem was resolved. Cecelia was a vampire who couldn't keep her man. And Lenore Society was a vamp who knew her way.

MONOPOLY

FOR DARBY DAY, BUSINESS-MAN, THERE ARE THE USUAL FOUR SEASONS PLUS A FIFTH... VAMPIRE SEASON. AND... DURING THAT ONE... HE HAS A...

DARBY DAY COULD NOT HELP THE FAILURE OF HIS PICKLE WORKS. HE HAD TRIED HIS BEST. BUT WHEN HE HAD TO LOOK AT THE RAMSHACKLE BUILDING, WITH ITS DELECTABLE SCENT OF SPICE STILL WAFTING OUTWARDS, HE COULD NOT HELP BUT THINK HE WAS SAYING GOOD-BYE TO A LONG, FAITHFUL FRIEND...

SO LONG... CHUM...

DARBY DAY VARIET

HEAD BOWED, DARBY DAY SHUFFLED THROUGH THE STREETS, NOT EVEN THE EVEN THE EXCITED SHOUTS OF FLEEING PASSER-BYS MENDED HIS BROKEN HEART...

VAMPIRES...

VAMPIRES!

VAMPIRES, SHAMPIRES! WHO CARES?

WHEN HE REACHED HIS APARTMENT HOUSE...AND HE WAS CLIMBING THE STAIRS TO HIS SINGLE ROOM...HE WAS STILL OBLIVIOUS TO ANYONE...OR ANYTHING...

GOT TO LOOK FOR A NEW BUSINESS...

NO VAMPIRE...IS...GET-TING ME!

HE SWITCHED ON THE LIGHT ONCE HE REACHED HIS ROOM. OUTSIDE, IT SEEMED LIKE A SMALL, YELLOW SQUARE OF PAINT...PALING WITH INATTENTION...

V-V-VAMPIRES!

BUT...WHAT--?

V-V-VAMPIRES! THAT'S IT!

AN IDEA HAD TAKEN HOLD IN DARBY DAY'S BRAIN. IMPATIENTLY, HE RAN TO THE BOOKSHELVES BEHIND HIM...HIS HAND REACHING OUT FOR A SINGLE BOOK...

WHY...WHY DIDN'T I THINK OF THIS SOONER? DARBY DAY...YOU'RE A FOOL!

VAMPIRES
REVISED EDITION

HE GRABBED THE WITHERED, DUSTY TOME, PLACING IT ON A TABLE BEFORE HIM. WILDLY, DARBY DAY FLIPPED ITS PAGES...MURMURING TO HIMSELF...

VAMPIRES? HMMM! VAMPIRES! LET'S SEE...VAMPIRES...AND THEIR...DEATH!

REACHING THE PLACE HE WANTED IN THE BOOK, HE SLAPPED IT DOWN ON THE TABLE. THEN, THROUGH THE NIGHT, HE STUDIOUSLY READ...

SILVER BULLETS! STAKES...THROUGH THE HEART! SEEMS TO BE THE ONLY WAY TO KILL THEM!

HA! WHY NOT? CAPITALIZE ON THIS VAMPIRE EPIDEMIC...BY MANUFACTURING...SILVER BULLETS...AND STAKES! HEH-HEH! A...SURE-FIRE SCHEME...TO KILL VAMPIRES...AND MAKE MONEY! I'LL HAVE A...MONOPOLY...ON IT!

IT WAS ALMOST TWO MONTHS LATER... TWO MONTHS OF HARD LABOR, WORKING ON HIS SILVER BULLETS AND TAPERED STAKES... THAT DARBY DAY DECIDED TO TRY OUT HIS PRODUCT IN THE LOCAL VAMPIRE CASTLE...

GULP.... THE PRICE OF FORTUNE...!

HE PENETRATED THE CASTLE'S SUFFOCATING DARKNESS, GOING DEEPER AND DEEPER INTO IT. SUDDENLY, DARBY DAY HEARD A SHUFFLE AND A THROATY, RAVENOUS GROWL. HE WHIRLED... READYING HIS GUN AND CROSS-BOW... TO FACE TWO VAMPIRES...

HEE-HEE-HEE HEE-HEE-HEE

YEOW! LET'S HOPE THESE THINGS ...WORK...!

FOR A MOMENT THERE WAS SILENCE. THEN HE SWUNG INTO CONCENTRATED ACTION. HIS GUN, HOLDING THE SILVER BULLET, SWEPT UP... AND FIRED...

BLAM!

THERE WAS A SCREAM. THEN EFFORTLESSLY, DARBY PLUCKED A FEATHERED, TAPERED STAKE FROM HIS SHEATH, APPLIED IT TO HIS CROSS-BOW... AIMED...

....AND LET LOOSE. THERE WAS A SPLIT-SECOND OF SINGING DEATH BEFORE THE STAKE STRUCK INTO THE CHEST OF THE SECOND VAMPIRE. IT WAS OVER.

BLOOoooM

MOMENTS LATER, DARBY DAY LOOKED DOWN UPON TWO FIGMENTS OF DEATH... WHO LAY BEFORE HIM... ONE WITH A BORE IN HIS CHEST CREATED BY A SILVER BULLET... AND THE OTHER WITH A CHEST FEATURING AN ALIEN FEATHERED STAKE...

IT...WORKS! IT WORKS!

VICTORIOUSLY, DARBY DAY HOISTED THE IMPLEMENTS OF VAMPIRE-DEATH ABOVE HIS HEAD. THERE, IN THE SHADOWS, HE LOOKED LIKE A KING WHO HAD COME HOME...

HA HA HA! IT WORKS! NOW... TO GO INTO... PRODUCTION!

IN A SMALL, MODEST WAY, DARBY DAY STARTED HIS VAMPIRE EXTERMINATING BUSINESS...

...AND THE FRIGHTENED PEOPLE RESPONDED...

...BUILDING HIS FIRM INTO BIGGER AND BETTER THINGS ...MUCH BIGGER...

...AND, AGAIN, THE SCARED PEOPLE RESPONDED!

DARBY DAY ADVERTISED HIS EERIE PRODUCT... ON THE ROAD...

...IN THE AIR...

SLOWLY, THE VAMPIRES WERE BEING EXTERMINATED. EACH NIGHT, ONE WOULD GET KILLED BY A DARBY DAY PRODUCT...

UNTIL DARBY DAY WAS A MADE MAN. THE PEOPLE HAD BOUGHT UP HIS SILVER BULLETS AND FEATHERED STAKES WITH AN INSANE FRENZY. DARBY, SEATED IN HIS PLUSH OFFICE, RELISHED HIS IMPORTANCE...

YOU CAN SEND IN THAT DELEGATION NOW, MISS HARRIS!

YES, SIR!

IN THESE PLUSH DAYS, DARBY HAD SEEN MANY DELEGATIONS. HE LOOKED AT THE THREE MEN ENTERING HIS OFFICE NOTICING NOTHING UNUSUAL ABOUT THEM...

GOOD DAY GENTLE-MEN!

GLAD WE...

...CAN GET...

...TOGETHER, MR. DAY!

HUMPH! YES, OF COURSE! WHAT CAN I DO FOR YOU?

THEN, SUDDENLY AN UGLY TRANSFORMATION TOOK PLACE IN THE THREE MEN. THEIR HAIR BECAME LONGER...THEIR EARS POINTIER...THEIR TEETH SHARPER. THEY BECAME RAVENOUS VAMPIRES...

YOU CAN...

...STOP...

...KILLING US!

THE THREE VAMPIRES LUNGED AT DARBY DAY. THEIR FANGS WERE BARED FOR THE THROATY KILL. DARBY QUICKLY GRABBED A GUN AT HIS SIDE...AND FIRED...

TH- THE GUN... IT DOESN'T WORK!

BANG!

BAM!

BAM!

CRASH

KRUMP!

HURRIEDLY, HE REACHED FOR THE LOADED CROSS-BOW. HE LET FLY A FEATHERED STAKE...BUT...

THE CROSS-BOW HAS FAILED! NO! NO!

THE VAMPIRES BACKED A QUIVERING, SLOBBERING DARBY DAY INTO A CORNER. HE COWERED, THE TASTE OF DEATH RANK IN HIS MOUTH. THE BLOOD-THIRSTY BEINGS LOOKED HUNGRILY AT HIS THROAT...TAKING TIME OUT TO ANSWER HIS QUESTIONS...

WHY DIDN'T YOU DIE? WHAT HAPPENED? WHY??!!

YOU SEE...

....MR. DAY...

....WE'VE GOT...

BULLET-PROOF VESTS ON!

THE END

5

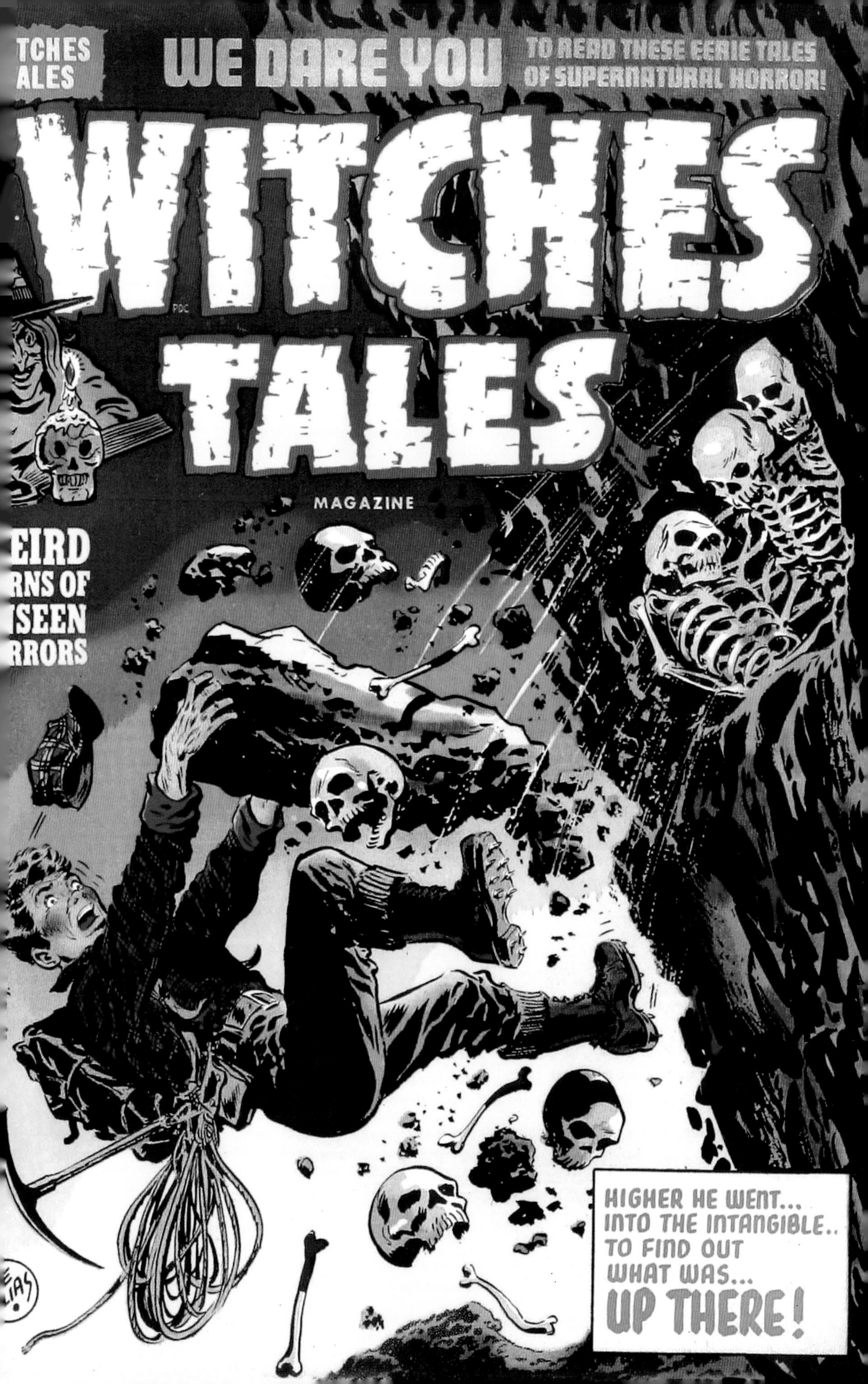
WE DARE YOU
TO READ THESE EERIE TALES OF SUPERNATURAL HORROR!
WITCHES TALES
MAGAZINE
HIGHER HE WENT...
INTO THE INTANGIBLE..
TO FIND OUT
WHAT WAS...
UP THERE!

WITCHES TALES, AUGUST, 1954, VOL. 1, NO. 26, IS PUBLISHED BI-MONTHLY by WITCHES TALES, INC., 1860 Broadway, New York 23, N. Y. Entered as second class matter at the Post Office at New York, N. Y., under the Act of March, 3, 1879. Single copies, 10c. Subscription rates, 10 issues for $1.00 in the U. S. and possessions, elsewhere $1.50. All names in this periodical are entirely fictitious and no identification with actual persons is intended. Contents copyrighted, 1954, by Witches Tales, Inc., New York, City. Printed in the U.S.A Title registered in U. S. Patent Office.

WELCOME

Dig in a messy grave and you'd find terror, wouldn't you? Well, that's what we offer! Crawl through a dark dungeon with time-gnawed walls and you're bound to come out shocked. Right? Well, we give you that feeling . . . plus! Look through these stories and you'll find the real thing . . . the intangible that makes your blood bubble and your eyes white. This is . . . TERROR!!

Every ounce of artificiality has been extracted . . . every particle of the synthetic has been subtracted . . . and every semblance of the unreal has been protracted. For in these stories, you'll find that distilled element . . . the kind that only makes for pure horror.

This is the "distilled element" that makes your reading matter different . . . that makes it unique . . . that makes it tense . . . that makes you come back for more. It's what you want.

And these yelling yarns are the kind that makes the small hours smaller . . . and has the chill of doom that only one cold, gray hand could create. These needling narratives have come to you from the nether region, where every step forward takes the reader to an acre that he should stay away from . . . but yet is compelled to go. These stories are different. They have the distilled element of fear!

WITCHES TALES

CONTENTS NO. 26

EVER FAINTLY, WARREN BUDD SMILED. THEN ROUTINELY...

TRUE, THERE IS NO EARTHLY REASON FOR THE FEELING. IT SEEMS TO BE ALMOST SUPERNATURAL. HOWEVER, I AM WILLING TO PUT MY...UHMM!...PROWESS TO THE TEST. SHALL WE SAY, I SHALL DIE...TO PROVE THAT I CAN'T?!!

1, 2, 3, 4, 5, 6, 7

CAN WE UNDERSTAND MR. QUIMBY'S ABASHED REACTION TO WARREN BUDD? CAN WE SEE WHY HE FELL INTO HIS CHAIR, SIGHING HEAVILY? I AM SURE WE CAN.

YOU SIGH, MR. QUIMBY, GOOD...VERY GOOD. IT SHOWS YOU ARE OVER YOUR INITIAL RELUCTANCE. MR. QUIMBY, THERE ARE FANTASTIC PROFITS TO BE MADE FROM MY...UHMM...GIFT. THEY CAN BE...ENORMOUS.

YOU'RE A LUNATIC!

BUDD WENT TO THE COAT RACK, HOLDING QUIMBY'S COAT OUT FOR HIM...

CALL ME WAH-WAH! ALL MY FRIENDS DO...! I THINK A BRISK WALK OUTSIDE WILL DO US BOTH GOOD. I'VE ALWAYS FOUND FRESH AIR QUITE CONDUCIVE TO BUSINESS. MUCH BETTER THAN A STUFFY OFFICE. SHALL WE GO?

Y...YES, OF COURSE. AIR...MUCH BETTER!

TO DESCRIBE MR. QUIMBY AS "TROUBLED" WOULD BE AN UNDERSTATEMENT. HE WAS, RATHER FRENZIED. OUTSIDE, WALKING BESIDE HIS TALKATIVE BOOKKEEPER, MR. QUIMBY FOUND THE SUNNY DAY AND COOL BREEZE SECONDARY TO THE CONVERSATION...

WAH-WAH, I HATE TO SEEM INQUISITIVE...BUT...COULD YOU TELL ME HOW YOU ACQUIRED THIS...UHMM...POWER OF NOT DYING? I DO HOPE I'M NOT PRYING.

NOT AT ALL, MR. QUIMBY. A RATHER CORRECT QUESTION AT THIS POINT, I SHOULD SAY.

REALLY, IT'S NOTHING ASTOUNDING. YESTERDAY MORNING I AWOKE...AND THERE I HAD IT. FELT RATHER STODGY...A STOMACH TIC...BUT I QUICKLY ADJUSTED. THAT'S ABOUT IT, MR. QUIMBY.

MAD-MAN-MAX YOUR FRIENDLY INSURANCE AGENCY

GUNS FOR HIRE

BUDD!

CRASH!

COULD IT HAVE BEEN A TRICK? A MIRAGE? COULD THE SAFE HAVE MISSED? MR. QUIMBY HAD TO ANSWER IN THE NEGATIVE. FOR THERE, IN FRONT OF HIM AND AS BIG AS LIFE, WAS WAH-WAH BUDD, ANALYTICALLY SHOOING AWAY A FLECK OF DUST FROM HIS SLEEVE...

2

WITH A BURST OF EMOTION, MR. QUIMBY GRABBED WARREN BUDD TOWARDS HIM, JIGGLING THE BOOK-KEEPER'S PINCE-NEZ...

SENSATIONAL, BUDD... ABSOLUTELY SENSATIONAL!

PLEASE, MR. QUIMBY... CONTROL YOURSELF! THIS IS SO UNLIKE YOU.

MR. QUIMBY RELEASED BUDD, STRAIGHTENED HIS TIE AND SUCCESSFULLY REGAINED HIS BUSINESS-LIKE COMPOSURE. BUDD SMILED...

UH...EXCUSE ME, WAH-WAH. IT... IT'S JUST THAT I GET SO EXCITABLE WHEN I SEE A CHANCE TO MAKE SOME... WHAT'S THE EXPRESSION... MOOLAH! B...BUT...CAN WE MAKE SURE? WILL YOU LIVE IN THE FACE OF... ANYTHING?

MOOLAH IT IS, MR. QUIMBY. AND... AS FOR SURETY....WELL, I THINK THAT CAN BE ARRANGED. IT REALLY IS AN EASY MATTER.

CORROBORATION, MR. QUIMBY...CORROBORATION! THEN, OFF WE GO.... TO A HUGE FORTUNE. HOWEVER, LET US HAVE SOME DINNER FIRST...AND TONIGHT YOU SHALL HAVE YOUR EVIDENCE, MR. QUIMBY. ...TONIGHT...!

MR. QUIMBY GULPED DOWN HIS MEAL. HE WAS NOT RAVENOUS; MERELY IMPATIENT. THAT NIGHT, IN A QUIET, DESERTED CARNIVAL, HE WATCHED AS WAH-WAH BUDD LED TO TO A HIGH-DIVE...

WAH-WAH, WHY DID YOU LEAD ME...HERE?

YOU WANTED PROOF, MR. QUIMBY. I AM GIVING IT TO YOU.

HE WATCHED AS WAH-WAH BUDD STARTED TO CLIMB THE LADDER. HE COULD HARDLY BELIEVE WHAT HE HEARD.

I WILL CLIMB THIS LADDER, MR. QUIMBY. I WILL CLIMB TO THE TOP...AND STAND THERE, MR. QUIMBY. THEN, I WILL JUMP INTO A...DAMP RAG! A DAMP RAG, MR. QUIMBY.

BUDD! DON'T BE AN IDIOT!

HE STOOD FROZEN AS HE SAW BUDD ATOP THE HIGH-DIVE, HIGH IN SPACE...

DO NOT WISH ME LUCK, I'M SURE I DON'T NEED IT!

BUDD.... WAIT! IT'S... FOOLISH... INSANE..!

THEN, WAH-WAH BUDD JUMPED...

3

BELIEVE ME NOW, QUIMBY?

POTZ! PLOTZ!

MR. QUIMBY COULD HARDLY BELIEVE HIS EYES. WOULD IT BE TOO MUCH OF A PUN TO SAY HE HAD "SEEN" ENOUGH? THE FORTUNE WAS THERE. NOW HE HAD TO GET IT...

AND THE MAN WHO HAD THE MONEY WAS JOHNNY YACHT, A MAN WHO WAS REFERRED TO IN RESPECTABLE CIRCLES AS A GANGSTER. HE WAS INDEED A MAN NOT AFRAID TO TAKE A CHANCE ON ANYTHING...

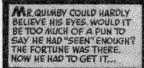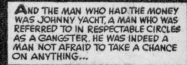

NOW... LET ME GET YOU STRAIGHT, QUILTY. YOU SAY YOU KNOW A GEEZER WHO CANNOT DIE?!! IS THIS RIGHT, QUEEZY?!!

QUIMBY IS THE NAME, MR. YACHT. YES, YOU ARE CORRECT. I AM WILLING TO PUT ALL THE MONEY IN MY POSSESSION... THAT YOU CANNOT KILL HIM.

3 MILE LIMIT

GAMBLING PERMITTED

COOLA

YOU HAVE CHEWED OFF A CHUNK, QUARTZ. IN UDDER WORDS, YOU WANT TO BET ME THAT I CANNOT KILL YOUR MAN. HOW'S ABOUT HUNNERT-THOUSAND, QUOOF?

(CAUGH) HUNDRED-THOUS..?!! GULP! (CAUGH!)

THIS IS MY OFFER, QUEEG! PUT UP... OR SHUT UP!

I... I ACCEPT, MR. YACHT! ONE MORE THING... THE NAME IS... QUIMBY!

I GOT IT QUIMTEE. OH, YES... I DON'T LIKE WELCHERS. MY FRIEND HERE DON'T LIKE WELCHERS. IN FACT, NOBODY LIKES WELCHERS. AM I UNDERSTOOD?

O... OF COURSE..!

AFTER HE LEFT JOHNNY YACHT, MR. QUIMBY FELT A LITTLE UNEASY. HE HAD A STAKE IN WAH-WAH BUDD. HE HAD TO MAKE SURE OF THAT STAKE.

I HAVE MADE THE WAGER, WAH-WAH. YOU CANNOT DIE. WHATEVER HAPPENS... YOU CANNOT DIE!

PLEASE, MR. QUIMBY, EASE YOUR MIND. I WON'T DIE!

4

COULD MR. QUIMBY HEAR IT? COULD HE HEAR THE GUN CLICK? YES, HE COULD. HE HOPED WAH-WAH BUDD WOULD LIVE UNDER WHAT HE KNEW WOULD BE A BARRAGE...

CLICK!

BAM! BANG! THUD WHAM CRACK! BUDD!

IF YOU DON'T DIE, I SWEAR I'LL KILL YA!

MR. QUIMBY WATCHED IT. HE SAW WHAT WAS NORMAL BUT, TO HIM, IT WAS THE ABNORMAL. HE SAW WAH-WAH BUDD CRUMBLE INTO A HEAP.

EASY AS PIE!

BUDD, YOU FOOL! YOU STUPID, IDIOTIC IDIOT! Y...YOU DIED! WHO TOLD YOU TO DIE? DID ANY-ONE GIVE YOU INSTRUCTIONS?

A SMILE SLIPPED INTO WAH-WAH BUDD'S FACE. HE WINKED...

TCH! TCH! TEMPERAMENT, MR. QUIMBY... TEMPERAMENT! I'M NOT DEAD!

BUDD! Y...YOU'RE... ALIVE! WHAT DID YOU DO? DO YOU REALIZE I LOST A FORTUNE TO JOHNNY YACHT?

DO YOU THINK MR. QUIMBY WAS SUR-PRISED AT WHAT WARREN BUDD WOULD SAY? YOU CAN BET YOUR SWEET LIFE HE WAS...

MR. QUIMBY, YOU'VE NO FORESIGHT. THE NEXT TIME...YOU'LL GET ODDS!

BUT... I HAVEN'T MONEY TO PAY HIM... NOW!

I HEARD YOU, QUIMBY! THAT WAS YOUR NAME, RIGHT?

BAM BLAM WHAM BOP CLICK BOOM WACK POW

TSK! TSK!

MR. QUIMBY, ONCE THE IMPORTER OF FINE LINENS, DIED. IN THAT THERE IS A MORAL, I SUPPOSE: NEVER TEAM UP WITH A MAN WHO CAN'T DIE! AND, AS FOR WARREN BUDD, HE LIVED FOREVER HAPPILY AFTER.

THE END

5

CHARLIE LOVES GOOD CAKES AND ALE,

CHARLIE LOVES GOOD CANDY,

CHARLIE LOVES TO KISS ALL THE GIRLS,

EXCEPT FOR MISS RANDY!

TWEEDLE-DUM AND TWEEDLE-DEE RESOLVED TO HAVE A BATTLE.

FOR TWEEDLE-DUM SAID TWEEDLE-DEE HAD SPOILED HIS NICE NEW RATTLE.

JUST THEN WALKED BY A MONSTROUS MAN AS BIG AS A TAR BARREL,

AND IMPRESSED BOTH THE HEROES SO, THEY QUITE FORGOT THEIR BATTLE!

THE PURSUIT

Hector McCloy still remembered the woman. He couldn't get her out of his head. Despite her good looks, the clear blue eyes as deep as quicksilver, the smart, pert dress, the velvety voice — despite these things, there was still something odd about her.

There, that day in his private detective's office, when she had given him all that money to track the man down, he recalled the strangeness about her. What was it?

He found the man. Some routine checking, putting together some odd facts, adding two-and-two, making the pieces fit, and he finally found him. That part wasn't too hard. The stiff part was knowing what the man looked like. How can a private detective really track a guy without knowing what he looks like? It was all so weird.

And there he was, no more than twenty-five feet ahead of him. McCloy had the man boxed into an alley. He didn't want it that way. You can't face a quarry when you're both boxed in: only one guy can leave. But he had no choice. The man had led him to this corner where there was no light. The moon wasn't even on his side. The heavy clouds, dragging across the sky like clods of damp rags, shrouded it. McCloy breathed silently. There was nothing. No, correct that! There were shadows, shuffling shadows — his and the man he hunted down.

McCloy slid the gun out from his shoulder holster. It felt firm, nice, in his hands. He always felt a hundred-percent better with a gun in his hand. Gives a guy a warm feeling of satisfaction. McCloy quivered, though. He had the gun; he hunted down the guy. Still, he was scared.

He edged forward, slicing the distance between him and the guy. Why doesn't he turn around? He gripped the gun with all his might, feeling the hard steel cut into the palm of his hand. He gritted his teeth. The time had come.

"NICHOLAS!" he called.

The man turned around swiftly. McCloy jumped. He had a light, an unearthly light, a crazy mixture of red and blue — and it was smack-dab in the middle of his forehead. It wasn't real.

The man shuffled forward, nearer to McCloy. The detective began to make out other assortments. The guy's face was metallic, like aluminum, and he had no mouth — just a microphone, a round one, that looked like an orange pushed into the face. He spoke:

"Leave, earthling!" It was no voice; just sound. McCloy went for the trigger, but he felt himself flying through the air, felt himself flat on his back, and the guy's cloyish, sickly fingers holding his wrists with the grip of a wrench. And McCloy was staring into that metallic face. It was horrible.

"You fool!" the guy said. "You fall for Marta's feminine wiles — and you find yourself confronted with a Martian!"

Marta! That was the girl's name, the weird girl. What did she have to do with a — Martian? The question was answered for him.

"You're going to die, earthling," the guy said, "for finding me out!" McCloy felt the blackness closing in, and before it was really black, he heard: "Didn't you know Marta was a Venusian? That Venus and Mars both have spies on Earth?"

WITHERING HEIGHTS

BLAST THESE MOORS!!! CAN GET LOST TOO EASILY!!

A BOO OF THE MONTH

THE FIGURE WAS LOST ON THE MOORS. THE DRIVING WIND AND BLINDING SNOWSTORM LASHED ABOUT HIM IN UNABATED FURY. A WARM LIGHT, BREAKING THROUGH THE STORM IN A YELLOW GLOW, DREW HIM ON, A BEACON OF SAFETY IN THIS HORRIBLE ENGLISH WEATHER...

1

THE FIGURE OPENED THE MASSIVE DOOR—CREST. HE FACED A WARM BUT CHEERLESS INTERIOR...AND A HANDSOME MAN...

GOOD EVENING TO YOU, SIR! THE MOORS ARE LONELY THIS TIME OF YEAR...LONELY AND MYSTERIOUS!

HOW SAY YOU, SIR? WHAT'S WRONG? YOU'RE AS PALE AS A SHEET!

I COULD HAVE SWORN...I HEARD A VOICE...OUT THERE ON THE HEATH! A...WOMAN'S VOICE...! THE WIND PLAYS TRICKS, THOUGH....!

~A WOMAN'S VOICE! TELL ME MORE!...YOU MUST...!

TH...THERE IS NOTHING... MORE! NOTHING, I TELL YOU! M...MY COACH BROKE DOWN... AND I'VE WANDERED HERE! MY NAME IS GREGORY PARSON! WHAT MORE CAN A STRANGER...SAY?!!

DID YOU SEE HER? SHE CALLED OUT MY NAME! TELL ME, MAN, DID YOU SEE HER?

SUDDENLY, AS IF HIT BY A STROKE, THE LANDLORD PUT HIS FACE TO HIS HANDS...AND SOBBED HEAVILY...

FORGIVE ME! I...I'M NOT MYSELF! I'VE BEEN ALONE SINCE SHE...CATHERINE...DIED! MY...CATHY...!

I...SEE! I'M VERY SORRY! BUT...IF YOU'LL SHOW ME MY ROOM, I'LL BE OBLIGED!

THE LANDLORD OF WITHERING HEIGHTS LED HIS LODGER TO HIS ROOMS. HIS FLICKERING CANDLE DARTED SHADOW PATTERNS ON THE COLD, GREY WALLS...

THIS WAY, SIR!

Y...YES! ...(GULP!)~

THEN, AS THE STRANGER ENTERED HIS ROOM AND SHUT THE DOOR BEHIND HIM, HEATH-CLIFF SOBBED INAUDIBLY. HIS WHOLE FIGURE WAS ONE OF DEJECTION AND DESPONDENCY...

CATHERINE...MY DARLING! COME BACK TO ME! CATHERINE, DARLING! CATHY...!

2

THE WIND RATTLED THE SHUTTERS OF THE HOUSE. IT MOANED HUNGRILY OUTSIDE. THEN IT CAME...SOUNDING LIKE A SIGH AT FIRST...THEN A MURMUR...FINALLY A NAME...

...HEATCLIFF... HEATCLIFF...!!

I HEARD IT! *HER* VOICE!

IT GOT LOUDER...

HEATCLIFF! HEATCLIFF!!

I'M COMING! I'M COMING, DARLING! CATHERINE!

HEATCLIFF!

I'M HERE, CATHERINE! *I'M HERE!*

HE RAN OUT SHOUTING! HE RAN OUT FLAILING THE WIND AND CRUSHING THE SCRAGGLY CARPET OF BLUE-GREEN GRASS UNDERFOOT. HE RAN, HAIR TOUSLED, CHEST HEAVING ARMS SWINGING, CALLING...CALLING TO HIS LOVED ONE!

CATHERINE! CATHERINE!

CATHY! ANSWER ME, DARLING! WHERE ARE YOU? CATHY! CATHY!

WHAT'S THE TROUBLE? CAN I HELP?

NO! I...IT'S JUST MY IMAGINATION PLAYING TRICKS ON ME, SIR! THE WIND HAS DECEIVED ME!

WELL THEN... GOODNIGHT!

AY! GOODNIGHT!

3

4

I COULDN'T SLEEP AT NIGHTS, CATHY. EVER SINCE YOU WERE TAKEN AWAY FROM ME, I KNEW YOU'D COME BACK! I KNEW IT SOMEHOW!

YES, DEAREST, I CAME BACK!

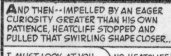

AND THEN--IMPELLED BY AN EAGER CURIOSITY GREATER THAN HIS OWN PATIENCE, HEATCLIFF STOPPED AND PULLED THAT SWIRLING SHAPE CLOSER...

I MUST LOOK AT YOU, DARLING, I'VE THOUGHT OF YOU SO MUCH-- SO MUCH!

NO, HEATCLIFF! NOT YET! I MUST TELL YOU SOMETHING FIRST--SOMETHING IMPORTANT!

IT CAN WAIT! LET ME LOOK AT YOU, CATHY. MY WONDERFULLY SWEET CATHY!

YOU WON'T LIKE WHAT YOU SEE, DARLING. I'VE... CHANGED. WE HAVE BEEN PARTED A LONG TIME!

BUT THE BURNING HUNGER OF REMEMBRANCE WAS TOO STRONG FOR THE GASPING MAN. HIS FINGERS DUG DEEP INTO YIELDING FLESH, SWINGING AROUND THE SHAPE OF HIS BELOVED...

I DON'T CARE! I MUST, DARLING! YOU'RE MY LIFE!

THEN LOOK--!

OH--H!

I TRIED TO TELL YOU, HEATCLIFF! I'VE BEEN DEAD, MY DARLING! DEAD--FOR YEARS! BUT I CAME BACK TO WARN YOU! NO--DON'T RUN AWAY FROM ME!

BUT HEATCLIFF BROKE AND RAN--HIS NERVE SHATTERED BACK TO REALITY. STILL THE THING PURSUED HIM TOWARDS THE VERY DOOR OF WITHERING HEIGHTS...

GET BACK! DON'T TOUCH ME!

DARLING! DARLING! I LOVE YOU! THAT'S WHY I CAME BACK TO SAVE YOU--TO TELL YOU ONLY WHAT THE DEAD KNOW. YOU'VE BEEN HOST TO... A...

--VAMPIRE!

AIIIIEEEEE!

THE END

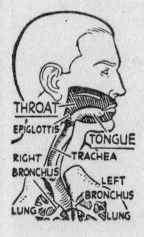

GET UP... AND GIVE IT THAT OLD COLLEGE TRY IN...

GO VAMPIRE

THE VAMPIRE, HAIR BEGINNING TO GRAY AROUND THE TEMPLES AND EARS, COULD HARDLY RESTRAIN A TEAR. HIS FANGED-MOUTH CURLED UP IN A SWEET SMILE AND HE RECALLED MEMORIES OF A BY-GONE DAY. SUDDENLY...

BY GUM, THEY REMEMBERED ROCKO-SOCKO SMITH BACK AT VAMPIRE U! THESE TROPHIES, WON THROUGH HARD WORK AND SWEAT, ARE TOKENS OF GLORY! NOW...ROCKO-SOCKO'S SON IS COMING HOME! MY BOY'S RETURNING...!

THE DOOR-BELL RANG. THE VAMPIRE RAN TO THE DOOR AND SWUNG IT OPEN...

HI THERE, DAD!

M-MY BOY... (GULP)...!

1

THE VAMPIRE LED HIS SON TO A MOTH-EATEN CHAIR. HE WATCHED HIM SIT DOWN. THERE WAS ENTHUSIASM IN THE FATHER'S VOICE...

THAT'S IT, BOY... REST! FOUR YEARS AT OLD VAMPIRE U. IS ENOUGH TO BUSH ANYONE! BY JINGO, I REMEMBER THOSE DAYS! YES SIRREE, THOSE CHEERS STILL RING IN THIS MIDDLE-AGED BRAIN! TIME CAN'T STILL *THEM!*

S-SURE, DAD..!

CHUKKA-CHUK...CHUKKA-CHUK...CHUKKACHUKKACHIN! BITE 'EM...BITE 'EM...RINTINTIN! GOOO, VAMPIRE! HOORAY, ROCKO....!

THE VAMPIRE SIGHED HEAVILY AFTER THE CHEER. HIS BREATH CAME HARD, BUT A NOSTALGIC SMILE WAS ON HIS FACE. HE LOOKED AT HIS SON, STILL SEATED IN THE CHAIR...

THAT'S HOW IT WAS BACK IN MY DAY, BOY! WE HAD FIRE! LOT'S O' SPIRIT! HOW'S THE NEW GENERATION AT VAMPIRE U.?!! THEY GOT THAT GET-UP-AN'-GO?

I--I GUESS SO, DAD..!

THERE WAS SOMETHING WRONG. THE SON'S FACE WAS BLANK EXCEPT FOR A TINGE OF ANNOYANCE. THE FATHER TRIED TO PERK IT UP...

WHAT'S WRONG, BOY? TIRED? WHERE'S THE OLD FIRE?

DAD, I-I'VE SOMETHING TO SAY. YO--YOU'D BETTER SIT DOWN.

SLOWLY, ALMOST CAUTIOUSLY, THE FATHER SAT DOWN...HE LOOKED UP INTO HIS SON'S SERIOUS FACE.

VAMPIRE U TAUGHT ME A LOT OF THINGS, DAD. I KNOW YOU HAD GOOD TIMES THERE...THE FOOTBALL GAMES...AND ALL THE RAH-RAHS! B-BUT, DAD...I LEARNED A GREAT DEAL THERE! I LEARNED WHAT I DIDN'T WANT TO DO... AND WHAT I WANTED TO DO!

GO ON, BOY!

I TRIED MY BEST TO CARRY ON IN YOUR TRADITION...TO GO IN MY FATHER'S FOOTSTEPS! BUT... I FAILED! YOU SEE, DAD... I JUST DON'T WANT TO BE A VAMPIRE!

VAMPIRE U. 40
VULCHER U. 32

SOLEMNLY, THE SON LOOKED DOWN. HIS FATHER JUMPED UP FROM THE CHAIR, PUT HIS ARM AROUND THE BOY, HUGGING HIM TIGHTLY...

THAT'S THE SPIRIT. I LIKE DETERMINATION. NOW,...YOU GO OUT THERE, BOY...AND DO JUSTICE TO VAMPIRE U.... AND DEAR OLD DAD!

B-BUT, DAD, I DON'T WANT...! OH, YOU DON'T UNDER-STAND..!

2

HIS ARGUMENTS WERE FUTILE, HIS PROTESTATIONS IMPOSSIBLE. THE FATHER COULD NOT SEE HIS SON'S VIEW. SO, THAT NIGHT, THE SON WENT OUT INTO THE DARK NIGHT, FEELING UNIMPORTANT IN HIS QUEST. HE HEARD THE CLICK-CLACK OF THE WOMAN BUT HE FELT NO ZEST IN WHAT HE WAS ABOUT TO DO...

SHE'S FRIGHTENED. WELL, THAT'S GOOD!

THE WOMAN WAS UPON HIM. HE JUMPED FROM THE SHADOWS...

YEOWW!

GO AHEAD, RUN! NOBODY'S GOING TO HURT YOU!

HE HOWLED BUT TO NO AVAIL. THE WOMAN RAN...AND THE SON SIMPLY WATCHED HER GO...

YOU DON' KNOW WHAT YOU'VE GOT, BOY: FIRE...VIM AND VITALITY! THAT'S YOUTH! DICKERDOO... DICKERDOO?...HOLLYHOLLYHOO! BLEED 'EM...BLEED 'EM...BOOBOO-BOOO! AH! THOSE WERE THE DAYS, BOY!

CAN I SAY SOMETHING, DAD...PLEASE?

THEN HE WENT HOME. HIS FATHER FACED HIM, PRIDE ON HIS FACE.

HOW'S THE BOY? GAVE 'EM THE OLD ONE-TWO, HUH? THAT'S THE SPIRIT. I LIKE THE OLD COLLEGE TRY! GAVE 'EM A NIP FOR VAMPIRE U!

DAD, I...I...!

HE WATCHED THE EXUBERANCE EBB FROM HIS FATHER'S FACE...

I HAD A VICTIM, DAD...A GIRL! B-BUT...I...I DIDN'T DO ANYTHING! SHE RAN!I JUST SAW HER RUN! I DIDN'T FOLLOW HER! I JUST SAW HER GO! DAD, I--I COULDN'T..! I DON'T WANT TO BE A VAMPIRE!

OH!

THE VAMPIRE GRABBED HIS SON, CLUTCHED HIM TO HIS BOSOM, THEN HE HELD HIM OUT AT ARM'S LENGTH, LOOKING AT HIM, THERE WAS ENCOURAGEMENT IN THE FATHER'S EYES...

NEVER MIND, BOY! WE'LL GO OUT THERE...AND SHOW THOSE PEOPLE WHAT A VAMPIRE FROM VAMPIRE U IS CAPABLE OF. UP WE GO, LAD...OUTSIDE...AND FOR A NIP.

B-BUT, DAD, I...I...! OH, ALL RIGHT..!

3

THE VAMPIRE AND HIS SON WALKED TO AN ALLEY. IT WAS QUIET, ALMOST SOMBER. AT THE ALLEY'S END THERE CAME A MAN. THE VAMPIRE TURNED TOWARDS HIS SON AND SPOKE TO HIM IN WHISPERS...

NOW, WATCH, BOY! HERE'S THE WAY WE DID IT BACK IN THE OLD DAYS!

YES, DAD...!

THE ELDER VAMPIRE SPRUNG...

THE VAMPIRE ACHED FOR THE MAN'S THROAT. BUT HIS INTENDED VICTIM FOUGHT BACK, BOTH LOOKING LIKE TWIN OGRES IN THE SHADOWS.

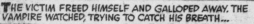

THE VICTIM FREED HIMSELF AND GALLOPED AWAY. THE VAMPIRE WATCHED, TRYING TO CATCH HIS BREATH...

UNN-H...HUFF! PUFF!

THE VAMPIRE TURNED TOWARDS HIS SON, WHEEZING, TRYING TO CONTROL HIS RAMPANT BREATH. THE SON MERELY SMILED...

COULDN'T...HUFF...QUITE GET THE RASCAL...(GROAN!) NOT WHAT...PUFF...I USED TO BE, SON! BUT...YOU GET THE IDEA, BOY! THAT'S THE WAY ROCKO USED TO GO... HUFF...AT IT!

I SEE, DAD! IT WAS A GREAT EXHIBITION!

SUDDENLY THE VAMPIRE LOOKED AT HIS SON. HE HAD NEVER SEEN HIM LIKE THAT...SO SERIOUS...SO UNATTENTIVE...

WH-WHAT'S THE MATTER, BOY?

I THINK IT'S ABOUT TIME I TOLD YOU, DAD!

TOLD ME....WHAT?!!

I TRIED TO SAY IT BEFORE...BUT YOU WOULDN'T LISTEN! YOU'VE GOT A PICTURE OF VAMPIRE U...AND I CAN'T CHANGE IT...NO MATTER WHAT I DO... OR SAY! WELL, DAD...VAMPIRE U'S CHANGED!

4

THE SON GREW SOMBER. HE HUNCHED HIS SHOULDERS. A VICIOUS SMILE CROSSED HIS FACE...

VAMPIRE U HAS KEPT ABREAST WITH THE TIMES. THINGS HAVE COME AND GONE! NEW THINGS HAVE TAKEN ITS PLACE. THE YOUNGER GENERATION IS TAKING OVER!

HOW DO YOU MEAN, BOY? VAMPIRE U WILL ALWAYS REMAIN THE SAME..!

YOU'RE WRONG, DAD! WE'VE LEARNED DIFFERENT THINGS! VAMPIRE'S ARE PAST! SOMETHING...SOMEBODY NEW...IS COMING!

THE BOY THEN TORE OFF HIS VAMPIRE WINGS...

FORGET YOUR CHEERS, DAD! NO MORE BITE 'EM! NO MORE BLEED 'EM..!

HE BLUNTED HIS POINTED EARS...

IT'S A NEW DAY... A GOLDEN DAY..!

HE RUBBED HIS HANDS OVER HIS FACE...

I OWE A LOT TO VAMPIRE U, DAD! A GREAT DEAL..!

THE VAMPIRE BACKED AWAY AS HIS SON CAME OUT OF THE SHADOWS. HE KNEW SOMETHING WAS CHANGED... SOMETHING HE NEVER SUSPECTED...

BOY... BOY... WHAT HAVE YOU DONE?

NO, DAD... NOT WHAT I'VE DONE! YOU SHOULD ASK... WHAT HAS VAMPIRE U TAUGHT ME... HOW THEY MADE ME PART OF A NEW AGE!

VAMPIRE U TOLD ME HOW TO BECOME... A ...GHOUL!

MY BOY, WHAT HAVE THEY DONE TO YOU!

THERE IS A MORAL TO THIS STORY. IT'S...VAMPIRES COME AND GO...BUT GHOULS ARE HERE TO STAY. SO... RAISE A CHEER! GHOULA ...GHOULA... The End

5

HUMPTY DUMPTY SAT ON A WALL,

HUMPTY DUMPTY HAD A GREAT FALL;

ALL THE KING'S HORSES AND ALL THE KING'S MEN

COULDN'T PUT HUMPTY DUMPTY TOGETHER AGAIN!

BIRDS OF A FEATHER FLOCK TOGETHER,

AND SO DO PIGS AND SWINE;

RATS AND MICE WILL HAVE THEIR CHOICE,

BUT I DON'T HAVE MINE!

FORTUNE HUNTER

Steve Thompson had figured it out perfectly. He wasn't going to let anyone stop him now. It was like a well-executed end-around-end football play, and he was carrying the pigskin for the touchdown.

Only the pigskin was a petite red-haired beauty, and the goal-line was the million dollars she was heir to.

He smiled as he thought of this imagery in football terms. It made his doings sound like true sportsmanship.

He was walking with his red-haired heiress now, passing a pleasant Sunday afternoon through the city's carnival. He put his arm around her, and she looked up at him.

"Oh, Steve," she said. "Just think of it. Only one more week, only seven more days."

"I wish it was today, Marsha," he said. "I hate every one of my days without you . . ." And your money, he finished silently.

She smiled her agreement. Then suddenly she became excited. "Oh look, darling! Look! A Gypsy fortune teller! Let's have our fortune told?"

"But, Marsha. You know that stuff is silly. It's nothing but a waste of time." A touch of fear had gripped him. Sure the stuff was a pack of lies, but what if that Gypsy really tipped her off? It was better if he played it safe.

"But, darling," she pleaded. "Just this once. I really want to."

Maybe it was better giving in this time, he decided. Show her what a compromising guy I am.

"I guess you can't say no to the woman you love," he lied so beautifully.

The Gypsy greeted them at the front of the tent. She showed them in and sat Marsha behind the crystal ball.

"I almost think she's going to tell me the truth," Marsha whispered to Steve.

"I'd kill her if she did," Steve told himself.

The Gypsy went to work. Her phoney mystic ways brought a smile to Steve's face. And her words made him feel even better.

"I see a great occasion coming into your life, young lady," she began. "I see a very lucky day coming your way. Why, it is just a week away. The two of you are there. There are many, many other people. Lots of friends and relatives. It is taking place in the city's biggest church."

Wow, is this a set-up, Steve thought. He could have kissed the Gypsy. Marsha reached for his hand. He smiled and kissed her on her forehead.

Yes, Steve Thompson was happy. Even the Gypsy was with him. At least, he thought she was.

For, you see, Steve Thompson had an accident that next week. And the following Sunday, a really lucky day in Marsha's life, there were many, many people at the city's biggest church. There were loads of friends and relatives of both Steve and Marsha. It was quite an occasion. It was . . . Steve Thompson's funeral.

YOU'D BLOW YOUR STACK IF YOU FOUND OUT WHAT WAS...

UP THERE

GENTLEMEN, ON THIS FILM IS MAURICE SHMEERZ'S SECRET. I PLAN TO SHOW IT TO YOU. UNFORTUNATELY, SHMEERZ IS NOT HERE TO SEE IT! HE IS...UMM...DETAINED!

DETAINED! A PSYCHIATRIST'S POLITE WORD FOR BEING COMMITTED. OH, EXCUSE ME! I'M MAURICE SHMEERZ. I CLIMBED LANAPURNA MOUNTAIN!

FOR THOSE WHO DON'T KNOW, LANAPURNA IS 29,602 FEET HIGH...AND IS THE MOST DANGEROUS OF THE HIMOLYA CHAIN! I...MAURICE SHMEERZ...AM THE ONLY MAN WHO REACHED ITS PEAK...WHO KNOWS WHAT'S...UP THERE!

1

"IT WAS ALMOST FIFTEEN MONTHS AGO THAT I SET OUT FROM MY NATIVE FRANCE...TO CLIMB LANAPURNA. THE FRENCH PRESIDENT WISHED ME GOOD LUCK..."

GOOD CLIMBING, MAURICE!

"MY WIFE WISHED ME GOOD LUCK..."

COME BACK SOON, MAURICE!

"MY FRIENDS WISHED ME GOOD LUCK..."

AU REVOIR, CHERI!

..MMMMM!..

"I WENT WINGING OFF TO THE HIMOLYA COUNTRY. THIRTY-SIX HOURS LATER I FOUND MYSELF IN A SMALL RUSTIC TOWN...WHERE I SHOOK HANDS WITH THE REST OF MY ASSOCIATES..."

WE'RE WAITING, MAURICE.

YES, MAURICE...AND SO IS...LANAPURNA!

"I TURNED AROUND...TO GAZE AT THE MIGHTY MOUNTAIN. SHE STOOD IN SPLENDOR...AN ALMOST INSURMOUNTABLE BARRIER. MY HEART POUNDED AS I SAW HER. YES, THERE SHE WAS...LANAPURNA!"

"IT TOOK US ALMOST TWO MONTHS OF SOLID PREPARATIONS BEFORE WE BEGAN THE CLIMB. BUT WHEN WE FINALLY DID START OUT, I KNEW WE LOOKED LIKE FOUR ANTS TRYING TO CONQUER A GIANT..."

"BUT, I, MAURICE SHMEERZ, KNEW THAT I WOULD DEFEAT HER. IT WAS MY DESTINY. WHAT I DIDN'T KNOW WAS...WHAT WAS UP THERE..."

2

"SOON, MY COMPANIONS AND MYSELF FOUND OUT THAT LANAPURNA WAS LIKE A FICKLE WOMAN. ONE MOMENT SHE WAS SWELTERING..."

"AND...8,000 FEET HIGHER...SHE WAS LIKE AN ICE-BOX..."

"FULL OF TREACHEROUS STREAMS AND DANGEROUS GULLEYS..."

"BUT I, MAURICE SHMEERZ, WAS ALWAYS ON HAND TO TAKE PICTURES OF THE DESTINY THAT WAS MINE."

"AT 10,000 FEET, THE GLARE OF THE SUN BOUNCING OFF THE SNOW WAS TREMENDOUS. WE HAD TO DON SUN GOGGLES TO PROTECT OUR EYES..."

"IT WAS SLIGHTLY HIGHER THAT WE EXPERIENCED AN AVALANCHE."

"BUT OFF WE SET AGAIN, UNDAUNTED...UNAFRAID..."

3

"IT WAS AT 16,002 FEET THAT I SAW THAT MY COMPANIONS DID NOT SHARE THE SAME DESIRES AS I. THEY WERE FRIGHTENED IN OUR PALTRY PITCHED-TENT THAT WAS SUPPOSED TO BE CAMP..."

I'M SORRY, MAURICE... FRANCOIS AND I CANNOT GO ANY FURTHER. WE'RE FRIGHTENED.

I SEE. AND YOU... MARIUS...ARE YOU FRIGHTENED, TOO?

NO, MAURICE, I WILL GO WITH YOU... TO THE TOP!

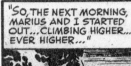

"SO, THE NEXT MORNING, MARIUS AND I STARTED OUT...CLIMBING HIGHER... EVER HIGHER...."

"SUDDENLY, THE ROPE THAT HELD MARIUS TO ME BROKE...AND THAT WAS THE LAST I SAW OF HIM ...."

YAAAAAA!

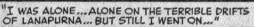

"I WAS ALONE...ALONE ON THE TERRIBLE DRIFTS OF LANAPURNA...BUT STILL I WENT ON...."

"I WAS EXHAUSTED. I COULD NOT BREATHE. I STRUGGLED TO REACH LANAPURNA'S TOP. THEN, AS IF BY MAGIC, I SAW IT...."

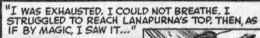

"LANAPURNA'S PEAK..."

"THE FIRST MAN TO REACH IT...THE THOUGHT RAN THROUGH MY HEAD. HIGHER I WENT...HIGHER... UNTIL I STOOD ON ITS SUMMIT...."

4

"ONCE ON TOP, I HEARD SOMETHING SNAP. I GUESS IT WAS MY MIND, FOR...ON LANAPURNA'S WINDBLOWN PEAK, 25,000 FEET HIGH...I FOUND OUT...FOUND OUT WHAT WAS ...UP THERE..."

HA..HA!
HA..HA
HA..HA!
HA..HA
HA
HA

"I COULDN'T RESIST THE TEMPTATION. I HAD TO TAKE MY MOVIES OF THE SCENE...TO SHOW IT TO THE PEOPLE. IT WOULD BE SOMETHING TO CONVINCE THEM... WHY I WENT CRAZY ON LANAPURNA..."

WELL, THERE YOU HAVE IT. THAT'S MY STORY...MAURICE SHMEERZ'S STORY. NOW... TAKE A LOOK AT WHAT THE PSYCHIATRISTS ARE GOING TO SEE~!

GENTLEMEN, WE ARE ON LANAPURNA MOUNTAIN NOW. MR. SHMEERZ TOOK THESE MOVIES. LET US SEE WHAT MADE HIS MIND GO!

WE ARE HIGHER NOW... NEARING THE PEAK!

NOW...WE ARE ON THE PEAK. LET US SEE ...

"I TOLD YOU. CAN YOU SEE WHY I WENT CRAZY CLIMBING LANAPURNA MOUNTAIN, AN *OLD FRANKFURTER STAND* WAS ...*UP THERE!*"

THE END.

5

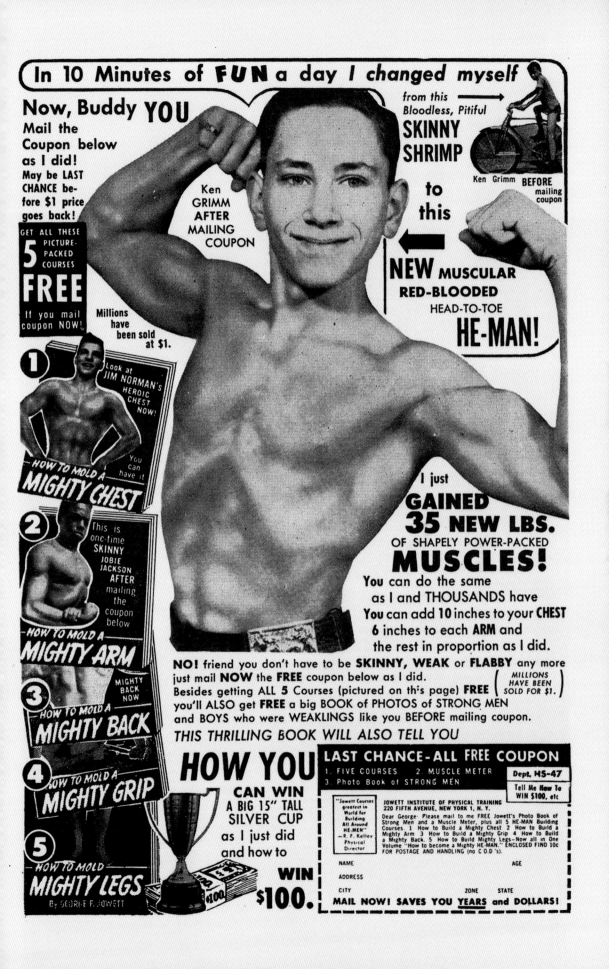

I really couldn't blame
The Other Girl

It was my own ugly skin that chased him away — but it was a Doctor's Formula that won him back

"Every time I looked in the mirror, I cried a little. I'd see my own awful skin blemishes and then I'd imagine Garth out with her. If only I could have smoother, clearer . . . yes, kissable . . . skin. How I wished I could win Garth back. Then my best friend told me her secret of Dr. Parrish's Double Jar Treatment. A Doctor's Secret, Juel's Be-Gone was such a quick, easy way. Ugly skin goes . . . in its place a new Loveliness . . . a new Life . . . at least that's what it meant for me. Now the skin he was ashamed of is the skin he loves to touch. Garth was mine again . . . completely.

The secret is in the 2 Doctor's Formulas that you, too, can use. Skin specialists agree that externally caused SKIN BLEMISHES CAN BE AVOIDED. They know the formulas and the method. The Doctor's 2 Jar formula was first prescribed in the Doctor's private practice. It worked such wonderful results that the Doctor's patients told their friends. They spread the good word. Now, all you do is follow the Doctor's directions and use these 2 formulas. The entire treatment takes only 3 minutes a day.

1. After you wash your face, you use Juel's Be-Gone Concentrated Special Cleansing Jelly. Your face, like your digestive tract, needs a thorough daily cleansing. Then this wonderful Jelly dissolves dry perspiration, pore clogging dirt, dust, grime. GIVES YOUR PORES A DEEP-CLEANING CONDITIONING.

2. Next . . . apply Juel's Be-Gone Fortified Skin Cream. Your skin needs the DAILY CARE to dry up pimple-causing blackhead plugs and speed healing. This Skin Combination prescribed by the Doctor gives abused neglected skin the special medicated care it needs. Help clean—condition—speed healing. Do this for 7 days. Then LOOK IN YOUR MIRROR. "Mirror, mirror on the wall — who is the fairest one of all?"

You can try Juel's Be-Gone Double Jar Treatment in your own home for a 10 day FREE TRIAL, and see the results on your own face. Imagine, Juel Be-Gone Double Jar Treatment is a formula prescribed by a Doctor, yet you get up to 25 *treatments for only* $2. Send no money, just send your name and address to *JUEL COMPANY, DEPT. B*, 1735 *West 5th Street, Brooklyn 23, N. Y.* NOW. When your Double Jar Treatment with the Doctor's simple, easy Directions is delivered, pay only $2. plus postage and handling charge. (or send $2 cash and you save C.O.D. and handling charges). You must be delighted or you may return it within 10 days and get every penny back — it's absolutely guaranteed. Remember, send your name and address to *JUEL COMPANY, DEPT B*, 1735 *West 5th Street, Brooklyn 23, N. Y.* Act quickly — so you can start sooner. Write Now. While your parcel is on the way to you, be sure to cleanse your face with warm water and rinse it with cold water as often as you can, as soon as you get your two jars — use them and prevent future miseries of bad skin.

Another story from the files of Dr. Edward Parrish, M.D., former New York State Health Officer, now consultant on all Juel Products.

WITCHES TALES

WE DARE YOU

TO READ THESE EERIE TALES FROM OUT OF THIS WORLD!

WITCHES TALES

THRILLING YARNS OF SUSPENSE

COULD HE STOP.....
THE THING THAT GREW?

WITCHES TALES, OCTOBER, 1954, VOL. 1, NO. 27, IS PUBLISHED BI-MONTHLY by WITCHES TALES, INC., 1860 Broadway, New York 23, N. Y. Entered as second class matter at the Post Office at New York, N. Y. under the Act of March 3, 1879. Single copies, 10c. Subscription rates, 10 issues for $1.00 in the U. S. and possessions, elsewhere $1.50. All names in this periodical are entirely fictitious and no identification with actual persons is intended. Contents copyrighted, 1954, by Witches Tales, Inc., New York, City. Printed in the U.S.A. Title registered in U. S. Patent Office.

THE Witch's MESSAGE

Heh! Heh! How many times the pot of evil has boiled! But, this time, the brew I have bubbling in it is special . . . it has ALL the ingredients of shrieking horror, savage suspense and blood-curdling action!

Never before have I gathered such a collection of tales. Never before has your sanity been called upon to withstand such terror as appears in this issue!

What is the secret of MURDER MANSION? Why do its walls tremble? Who does the dance of death?

Then, in THE THING THAT GREW, you will see right before your bulging eyes a monster that defies nature. You will find yourself twisting from under its deadly foot as it tries to crush thousands. A tidal wave could have no greater fury.

But, can there be a greater mad-masterpiece of horror than the SERVANTS OF THE TOMB? See dead men walk, giants battle, and thousands riot in panic! Cringe when the Tomb of Zombies is opened!

Heh! Heh! Wait! There is more! Read about the two who thought they could know the mysteries of the unknown. Read what happens when they meet the Frogmen!

Heh! Heh! Heh! You can't wait, can you? Very well, turn the page and take the journey through fear!

The creatures who rule the DEAD did not sleep quietly beneath the ROTTING house! They reached from another world, calling through the shadows, waiting... waiting to claim tenants for the...

MURDER MANSION

LUCY AND JERRY WILLIAMS SPED THROUGH THE NEW ENGLAND NIGHT TO SPEND THEIR HONEYMOON IN LUCY'S FAMILY MANSION— A HOUSE SHE HAD INHERITED...A HOUSE SHE HAD NEVER SEEN!

OH, DARLING, I HOPE WE LIKE MOON MANSION.

IT'S PROBABLY A SWEET LITTLE PLACE... AND IT'S ALL OURS!

BUT AS THE YOUNG COUPLE WENT OUT INTO THE NIGHT AIR, LUCY WAS UNEASY! A SOLITARY CAB DRIVER WAS THE ONLY FIGURE IN THE DESERTED DEPOT...

WHAT A DREADFUL PLACE! WHAT A QUEER OLD MAN!

HERE WE ARE, DARLING...OH, DRIVER! CAN YOU TAKE US TO MOON MANSION?

I DON'T GO TO MOON MANSION! THE DEVIL LIVES THERE—IT'S HA'NTED! YE KIN WALK UP THE ROAD TO GIT THERE, BUT IF YE WANT TO LIVE—STAY AWAY FROM MOON MANSION!'

AS THEY WALKED THROUGH THE BLACKNESS, LUCY FELT TERROR GROWING WITHIN HER...AND THEN, AFTER A SUDDEN BEND IN THE ROAD...THERE LAY MOON MANSION, GHASTLY IN THE MOONLIGHT!

OH, OH, JERRY! I—FEEL THERE'S SOMETHING EVIL ABOUT THIS PLACE!

NONSENSE! IT—IT'S JUST THAT THE OLD MAN FRIGHTENED YOU!

LATE THAT NIGHT, WHEN THE EVIL HOURS WERE AT THEIR DARKEST, LUCY WAS AWAKENED BY SOUNDS THAT SEEMED TO COME FROM...ANOTHER WORLD!

COME! COOOOME!

WHO'S THERE! WHO LIT THE FIRE IN THE STOVE? JERRY! JERRY! WAKE UP!

JERRY! THERE—THERE'S SOMETHING IN THIS ROOM! I CAN FEEL SOMETHING WATCHING US!

WHA-? WHAT'S THE MATTER? THERE'S NOTHING HERE!

CO·O·O·ME...COME LUCY-Y-Y-Y!

SEE? I TOLD YOU THERE'S NOTHING HERE...YOU'RE JUST JUMPY, DARLING, BECAUSE OF THE DARKNESS...

I CAN FEEL THEM WATCHING ME IN THE BLACKNESS! THEY'RE CALLING...CALLING!

THE VOICES ECHOED IN LUCY'S BRAIN! SHE FELT THE CREATURES OF DREAD PRESSING TOWARD HER THROUGH THE SHADOWS...

NOW YOU JUST GO TO SLEEP, DARLING...I WON'T LET ANYTHING HURT YOU!

JERRY...IF WE DON'T LEAVE...YOU-YOU WILL REGRET IT...I FEEL THE TOUCH OF DEATH IN THIS ROOM!

WHEN MORNING CAME, LUCY WAS SURE THAT THE VOICES HAD BEEN A NIGHTMARE! BUT WHEN THEY WENT TO THE GENERAL STORE...

SO YE BE THE ONES WHO LIVE IN THE *BLACK PLACE*...? HEE, HEE, 'TIS A PLACE OF *TERROR*.!!

OHH, JERRY!

TELL ME, OLD WOMAN, WHY DOES EVERYONE HERE FEAR MOON MANSION?

IT WAS BUILT OVER A *CEMETERY*.! HEE HEE! THE CREATURES OF THE *GRAVES* ROAM THE ROOMS OF THE MANSION! RUN AWAY, I TELL YOU, *RUN! RUN!*

AS THE CLOUDS OF NIGHT COVERED THE MANSION, LUCY ONCE MORE FELT SOMETHING CALLING TO HER... FOREVER CALLING!

A CEMETERY! I MUST FIND OUT WHAT IS DOWN THERE... BEFORE I GO OUT OF MY MIND!

YAWWNN! I'M GETTING TIRED, LUCY! I'M TURNING IN!

ALMOST HYPNOTIZED, LUCY WAITED UNTIL HER HUSBAND LEFT THE ROOM...THEN, TAKING THE LAMP, SHE WALKED TOWARD THE CELLAR DOOR---

I- HEAR- YOU! I AM COMING! I AM COMING!

I- I SEE NOTHING! NOTHING! *WHAT* IS DOWN THERE!

IN THE *TOMBLIKE SILENCE* THAT FOLLOWED THE ECHOES OF LUCY'S VOICE, A DOOR OF A *HIDDEN CRYPT* SWUNG OPEN! THE LEGIONS OF THE *LIVING DEAD* SWARMED BEFORE HER EYES...AND REACHED OUT...AND TOOK HER!

IT'S A *GRAVE*...IT'S *HORRIBLE*...IT'S- OH, NO *NO NO NO!*

NO—DON'T—ARRRGHH!

THE SCREAMING DARKNESS OF THE PIT CLOSED OVER LUCY, AND WHEN SHE EMERGED, SHE WAS A WALKING CORPSE...A WITCH OF EVIL!

NOW I KNOW WHAT CALLED ME...HEE HEE! I MUST—KILL! I—MUST KILL—JERRY—HEE! HEE! HEE!

JERRYYY...JERRYYYYY...I AM COMING UP TO YOU NOWWW...

WHA—! WHO IS THAT? LUCY——WHERE ARE YOU, LUCY?!!

LUCY! WHAT'S THE MATTER?? YOU LOOK SO STRANGE! YOU LOOK SO DIFFERENT! WHAT'S HAPPENED...LUCY!!

IT'S ALL RIGHT NOW, MY DARLING...JUST LET ME PRESS THIS LITTLE BUTTON! HEE, HEE!

STOP! THE BED....IT'S GOING TO CRUSH ME...YOU'RE NOT LUCY! WHAT ARE YOU? STOP!!

THIS IS WHAT CALLED ME, MY DARLING...DEATH! HA HA HA HARRGH! DEATH! DEATH!

LIKE A HORRIBLE VISE, THE BED CANOPY LOWERED, BRINGING THE CRUSHING SOUNDS OF BLOODY DEATH!

NO! NOOORRRGRGG...

HA HA! MOON MANSION IS NOT FOR THE LIVING! IT SHALL BE THE HOME OF DARKNESS UNTIL THE DAY OF DOOM!

WHERE BE YER HUSBAND, MRS. WILLIAMS?

HE HAD TO GO AWAY—BUSINESS! *HEE HEE!* GIVE ME MY THINGS AND LET ME GO!

WHY WOULD THEY WANT TO LIVE IN THE BLACK PLACE? MY, BUT SHE ACTED STRANGE-LIKE!

ENCLOSED IN THE BLACKNESS OF MOON MANSION, LUCY CALLED TO THE *SPECTERS* THAT *HAUNTED* THE MUSTY ROOMS OF *DEATH*...BUT...

COME TO ME, *SPIRITS OF EVIL!* COME FOR HOURS OF...*WHA-*? WHO COULD BE CALLING HERE...!

KNOCK! KNOCK!

WHO ARE YOU? WHAT DO YOU WANT HERE AT THIS TIME OF NIGHT?

THE PEOPLE IN THE VILLAGE TOLD US THIS PLACE IS FOR SALE...MAY WE COME IN? IT'S A BAD NIGHT!

I DON'T LIKE THIS PLACE, JOHN...IT SCARES ME!

HUSH, DEAR, SHE'LL HEAR YOU!

THEY LIED TO YOU! THERE IS SOME MISTAKE! THIS PLACE IS NOT FOR...YOU! PLEASE GO!

BUT THE "THINGS" HAD COME AT LUCY'S CALL! EVEN THOUGH SHE COULD NOT SEE THROUGH THE SHADOWS THAT CLUSTERED ABOUT LUCY, THE WOMAN COULD SENSE THE *PRESENCE OF EVIL*...

EEEEEE—JOHN! I THOUGHT I SAW SOMETHING BEHIND HER... SOMETHING *HORRIBLE*...TAKE ME AWAY!

WHA-! PLEASE, DEAR, IT'S JUST THE LIGHTNING!

THEY HAVE SEEN THE POWERS OF THE MANSION... THEY MUST NOT LEAVE HERE ALIVE!

PLEASE CALM YOURSELVES...THERE IS NOTHING HERE! IF YOU WILL EXCUSE ME FOR A MOMENT...!

WHILE THE VISITORS WAITED, LUCY PRACTISED THE BLACK ARTS! HER PURPOSE WAS THE PURPOSE OF... MURDER!..

SLAVE-SPIRIT OF MY MURDERED HUSBAND! OUTSIDE IS THE CAR IN WHICH THE VISITORS HAVE COME...DESTROY IT! LET THEM NOT ESCAPE THE TOMBS OF MOON MANSION...

IT...SHALL BE... DOOOOONE...

CRASH! CR-RACK

WHAT HAPPENED!

OUR CAR...OUR CAR HAS BEEN DESTROYED BY LIGHTNING!

OH, JOHN... I'M FRIGHTENED!

YOU HAD BEST STAY HERE...IT'S A WILD NIGHT! I ONLY HAVE TWO BEDROOMS THAT CAN BE...USED! BUT, ONE OF THE GIRLS WILL HAVE TO STAY IN MY ROOM!

AFTER SOME ARGUMENT, LUCY CONVINCED HER GUESTS TO STAY! IN THE MIDNIGHT BLACKNESS SHE LAY RIGID, IN AN OCCULT TRANCE... CALLING OUT A SPELL OF DOOM...

NOW, SISTERS OF DARKNESS! NOW! TAKE THESE MORTALS THAT HAVE INVADED OUR HOUSE...CRUSH THEIR BODIES!

THE *FURIES OF THE DEAD* AROSE TO LUCY'S CALL! IN THE NEXT BEDROOM, THEY TORTURED THE MINDS AND BODIES OF THE VISITORS...

JOHN! THERE IS SOMETHING HERE! WHAT IS THAT *BLUE LIGHT?* OH, MY BODY ACHES SO...SUCH TERRIBLE PAIN...HELP ME, JOHN!

WHAT IS IT? WHAT'S THE MATT--LOOK! THOSE *HIDEOUS EYES!*

AIYEEE!... I CAN'T STAND IT! HELP! THE PAIN...*THE PAIN! ARRRRR...* HELP MEEEE...

STOP! *STOP!*...OH! MY HEART...MY HEART... ARGGGHHHGGHGH!

DIE! DIE! DIE!

MOON MANSION HAD CLAIMED BLOOD AGAIN...

AND IN THE BEDROOM OF THE GIRL WHO SLEPT ALONE, THE *SMELL OF DEATH* ALSO ENTERED! LONG SPIKES *SILENTLY SLID* OUT OF THE WALLS MAKING THE ROOM A *CHAMBER OF HORRORS...*

WHAT IS THAT FIRE? I MUST GET OUT OF HERE...FATHER! MOTHER! HELP! *HELP!*

BUT THE GIRL'S MOTHER AND FATHER WERE *BEYOND* HELPING ANYONE! THE GIRL RACED TOWARD THE POINTS OF *MURDER,* THE SLENDER SPIKES SHE DID NOT SEE...

EEEEEEE! THE FACES! THE *HORRIBLE* FACES... I *MUST* GET OUT OF HERE...HELP! HELP!

EEEEEEEEE-*UGH!*

AND IN LUCY'S BEDROOM, THE OTHER GIRL SAT UP, WIDE AWAKE WITH *SUDDEN TERROR!*

EEEEEEE-*UGH!* WHAT WAS THAT *SCREAM!?* THOSE FLAMES...WHERE ARE THEY COMING FROM?!

AS SHE SPRANG FROM THE *BED OF DEATH,* THE GIRL ACCIDENTALLY TOUCHED THE *SECRET BUTTON!*

WHAT IS THAT IN THE BED?!! I MUST BE *LOSING MY MIND!!* NO! NO! THOSE FLAMES...

LUCY WAS KILLED! KNOCKING OVER THE CANDLE, THE GIRL RAN FROM THE ROOM LIKE A *SHRIEKING TORCH!*

THE BED....IT *KILLED* HER! OH! OH! THE CANDLE! I'M *BURNING*...NOOO! NO! EEEEYAAAHHH!

EEEYAARGHH!

THE MANSION OF THE DEAD BECAME A MASS OF *DEVOURING FLAME*...THE VILLAGERS CAME TOO LATE TO STOP THE FIRE, AND AS THEY WATCHED THE DESTRUCTION OF THE *BLACK PLACE*...

YAAAAAAAAAOOOOOOOOO!

THE SCREAM OF *DEATH!*

WHAT WAS THAT?

I TOLD THEM NOT TO GO THERE... I FEEL SORRY FOR THE YOUNG COUPLE! WHAT A WAY TO DIE!

THE HUSBAND WAS AWAY... T'IS THE *LASS* I FEEL SORRY FOR! SHE WAS SO *YOUNG* AND *SWEET!* BUT AT LEAST THE BLACK PLACE IS *NO MORE!* IT WAS A *MURDER MANSION!*

THE END

WHAT ARE THE *APPALLING* CREATURES THAT EMERGE FROM THE WILD, BEATING HEART OF THE SWEATING JUNGLE?... WHY DO EVEN THE BEASTS SHRIEK IN TERROR AT THE SIGHT OF THE...

GREEN HORROR

DEEP IN THE JUNGLES OF BRAZIL, WHERE HUMANS SHOULD NOT *DARE* TO VENTURE, WHERE *FEAR* AND *DANGER* WAIT BROODING IN EVERY CORNER, TWO PEOPLE MOVE SLOWLY TOWARDS A PERILOUS ADVENTURE...

HURRY, RUTH!! THAT RIVER SHOULDN'T BE VERY *FAR* NOW!!

I'M TIRED, FRANK! I STILL DON'T BELIEVE THOSE *FROG MEN* REALLY EXIST!!

THIS MUST BE IT!! WE CAN CAMP BY THE BANK!

I DON'T LIKE IT, FRANK!! THE WATER LOOKS SO... *STRANGE!!*

WHEN DAY COMES, THE EXPLORERS LOOK AGAIN AT THE *MYSTERIOUS* RIVER...

I MUST ADMIT THE RIVER LOOKS *BETTER* THIS MORNING! AND I DON'T SEE ANY OF YOUR *FOOLISH* FROG MEN ABOUT!!!

I GUESS I DRAGGED YOU ON THIS EXPEDITION FOR *NOTHING*, RUTH! BUT THOSE *SECRET RECORDS* SAID THEY EXISTED---

THINK I'LL GO IN FOR A SHORT SWIM! WANT TO COME, "PROFESSOR"?

NO, I WANT TO LOOK OVER THESE MAPS. WE MIGHT HAVE THE *WRONG* RIVER!!

OH, WHAT I HAVE TO GO THROUGH BEING THE WIFE OF AN EXPLORER... *IS THAT YOU, FRANK??*

*S*UDDENLY, A *REPULSIVE* CREATURE, *HALF-MAN, HALF-FROG*, APPEARS IN THE WATER, ITS WEIRD VOICE RAISED IN A *CHILLING* CHANT OF *DEATH!*...

FRANK!!! HELP!!! HELP!!

KRAAGHHH-HHH.!! KRAAAGGHH-HH.!!

A *HUMAN FROG!* I'M COMING, RUTH!!

AHH-H-H..

KROWWGG-HH-H-H-H!

KILL HIM, FRANK!!!

AWRRRGHH-H-H-H-H!!

THE END.

ONE MILLION *VOLTS!*

"Do you have anything to say?"

"Get it over with, you stinking cops!"

"Put the head-piece on."

"Ready, Warden."

"When the red light goes on above the chair, you know what to do."

The red light blinked on.

ZZZZZZZZIIIIII!!!!

"Warden, look. He's glowing!"

"More electricity."

"We've got it up to a million volts now, sir."

"Something has gone wrong. Oh no! He's getting up ... he's ripping the straps."

The police in the electrocution room huddled against the walls. Standing before them, his body bristling with electricity, was Pretty Boy Wills.

Finally, the warden found his voice.

"Everyone out of here. We'll lock him in."

Everyone tried to escape the monster at once. They jammed at the door but before they could all get out, Wills had staggered over and grabbed one of the policemen.

"Quick! Slam that door shut!"

The warden and the others clustered around the window, looking in on the room. Their minds were confused ... almost frozen with horror.

"Look! He's got Lewis. He's holding him in his arms. The electricity from his body is burning Lewis to a crisp!"

"Doctor," gasped Warden Trent, "what happened?"

"I don't really know, but I think his body somehow has absorbed the electricity and is using it as we would blood. It's a medical miracle ...Watch out! Get away from these metal walls!"

The doctor's warning came just in time. Wills was nearing the door. The minute he touched it, the walls became charged with deadly electricity.

"What do we do now?" shouted one of the attendants, "he's battering down the door!"

No one could move! If Wills got out, he would never be stopped. Suddenly, the sound of sizzling electricity behind the door stopped. The walls were no longer charged.

"Open the door," ordered the doctor. The huge door swung open. The men fell back in terror.

"Just as I thought," exclaimed the doctor, "our bodies are only so strong. After several minutes the electricity finally killed him."

The doctor pushed his foot through the pile of dust that had once been a man!

DUEL AT DAWN !

"The sun's hot."

"Yeah. These bags are getting heavy."

"Quite a place, this canyon."

"It's gonna take some traveling to get out o it."

"Just think, Spider, we've got enough gold in these bags to make us millionaires."

"I been thinking about that, Joe. Look, why don't you throw that gun away. It makes me nervous."

"This gun makes me feel safe, Spider. You were okay — helping me kill that prospector who struck it rich and getting his gold — but that's done. Now, you'd slit me in two to get all the gold!"

And so the two men rode on. As the days passed the friction between them increased. Joe knew he needed Spider to lead him out of the Gold Mountains. Spider knew he could have everything if he could get the gun.

When they bedded down for the nights, they tried to fight off sleep in order to watch each other. One night....

"Just a little more ... little more ... oops...."

Spider had kicked loose some stones as he crawled towards Joe. The other murderer fell back with a start.

"So, you tried to finish me! Looks like I don't get to sleep anymore."

"Aw, look, Joe, I'll tell you what. Give me three quarters of the gold an' I won't touch you."

"No!"

More hot, dust-filled days passed. Now both men did not dare to sleep. One wanted to kill. The other wanted to live.

Spider was the bigger and stronger of the two. He knew that sooner or later Joe would have to give in. His chance came.

Night wore on to dawn. Joe, his face drawn, his brow fever-charged, could barely keep awake. Suddenly, he pitched forward, unconscious.

With a mad lunge, Spider was upon him, his hands ripping the gun from Joe's.

"Now, I got him."

Spider rose and backed away a few feet. He leveled the gun at Joe's head.

BLAM!

Spider began to laugh insanely. Then, his laughter changed to shrieks of terror. The vibrations set up by the gun's explosion had started a landslide!

Tons of rock began to cascade down the canyon walls. In minutes, Spider was crushed under the avalanche. Just then, the sun rose and its rays caught a small piece of ore. It sparkled—the last remains of a buried treasure!

SAVAGE AUSTRALIAN BOOMERANG

The SECRET of the WILD BUSHMAN

IT ALWAYS COMES BACK

The amazing "Flying Stick" was originally made by the Wild Savages of Australia. They used it as a weapon against their natural enemies and to hunt and kill birds and animals. They discovered the secret of shaping and throwing the BOOMERANG so that it would always fly to the place they aimed at and then come back to them!

NOW—YOU CAN LEARN THIS ANCIENT SECRET

One of the oldest sports in the world, this is the modern style of the age-old weapon of the Australian Savages. It flies on the same principle as a modern airplane. With this wonderful BOOMERANG, you can find out how the Wild Men did this trick. We can tell you this much now—part of the secret is in the wrist!

When you throw the BOOMERANG, it spins out and away in a big circle. It's Amazing! No matter how far or how high or how hard you throw it—it always comes back! Try it in your own backyard or when you go hunting. A little practice gives deadly accuracy.

WONDERFUL FOR HUNTING, TARGET PRACTICE

Almost any object, a rabbit hiding behind a stump or a bird on the wing, is a mark for the flying stick. Or try hitting a balloon floating in the air. If you miss, the BOOMERANG comes back to you like a trained eagle, ready for another flight. Fine as a shotgun target and a new way of teaching your dog to "fetch". Comes with Full Instructions.

DELUXE MODEL BOOMERANG $2.49

Flight-tested—Larger, Stronger, more Accurate, 17-inch wing spread—flies a 225-ft arc. Carved from special Waterproof Laminated wood—finished in brilliant Jewel colors.

$1.00

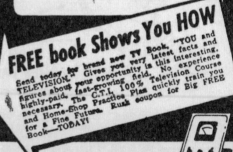

No person dares to think what *FOUL* and *UNNATURAL* horrors lurk beneath the black surface of the earth waiting to crush human life between their slimy fingers... yet of all these monsters none are so *APPALLING*, so *TERRIFYING* as the...

SERVANTS OF THE TOMB!

Under an age-old tomb in *WESTERN ASIA*, a group of *WEIRD* figures wander endlessly. They are being *PUNISHED* for their *HORRIBLE CRIMES* while free...

OH-H-H!! OH-H-H-H!!

WE ARE DOOMED *NEVER* TO SEE THE *LIGHT* AGAIN!!!

WE EXIST ONLY TO PREPARE FOR BURIAL THE *CORPSES* THAT ARE TO REST IN THE TOMB ABOVE!!

WE CAN *NEVER* LEAVE THIS ROOM!! *NEVER*!!

OH-H-H-H-H!!

---AND TONIGHT THE FULL MOON *APPEARS!* IF WE CAN BRING ITS LIGHT IN *HERE,* THE BODY WILL BE RESTORED TO *LIFE!!!*

AND WE CAN LEAD HIM AGAINST *THOSE* WHO LOCKED US IN THIS DUNGEON *FOREVER!!*

THE STONES IN THE WALL HAVE BEEN *LOOSENED* BY BEING CONSTANTLY BROKEN DOWN! WE CAN *ESCAPE--* WITH TORO AS OUR *LEADER!!!*

YES! YES! LET US *HURRY!*

NO! WE CANNOT OPPOSE THE GODS BY RESTORING THE DEAD TO LIFE!! IT IS AGAINST THEIR *WISHES!!!* WE ARE JUST *TOMB SERVANTS!*

THAT IS TRUE! WE WILL BE *SEVERELY PUNISHED!!!*

IN A MOMENT, *FIERCE* WORDS STRIKE OUT LIKE COBRAS IN THE DARK AND THE AIR IN THE ROOM BECOMES HEAVY WITH *DANGER* AND *FOREBODING...*

DO YOU WANT TO *ROT* HERE FOR THE REST OF YOUR DAYS?

THE GODS WILL UNLEASH THEIR WRATH UPON US FOR DISTURBING THE *DEAD!!*

THEN WE WILL DO IT *WITHOUT* YOU!! DIE, FOOL!!!

EIRG-H-H-H-H!!!

AIRGH-H-H-H!!

N-AH-H-H-H!!!

THE BATTLE BEGINS... RAWRRRR!! GRAWRRR!!

YOU *MUST* WIN, TORO! YOU *MUST*!!

AWRRRrrr!!!

DIE AT LAST, MONSTER OF *EVIL*!!!

ARRGHH·H·H!!

FREE FROM THE THREAT OF *SUDDEN DEATH*, THE PEOPLE TURN WITH FURY ON THEIR ASSAILANTS...

WHY DON'T WE KILL THEM. THEY DESERVE NO BETTER!

YES! WE'LL SHOW THEM WHAT IT IS LIKE TO FACE DEATH WITHOUT WARNING!!

NO, PEOPLE, YOU MUST NOT KILL THEM. THEY MUST RETURN TO THEIR *PRISON* BENEATH THE TOMB--- *NEVER* TO LEAVE AGAIN!

AND SO THE TOMB SERVANTS RETURN TO THEIR VAULT, FOREVER SHUT FROM THE LIGHT OF THE SUN, FOREVER DOOMED TO LIVE WITH THE *DEAD*!

THE END.

THE VAMPIRE'S RETURN

"George, move the lantern closer to the coffin!"

The yellow, misty light fell fully upon a rusting red coffin. A huge triangular shield could be seen on one side of the decaying box. On the shield was inscribed . . .

"HERE LIE THE REMAINS OF THE HUMAN VAMPIRE. THE WOODEN STAKE THAT PIERCES ITS HEART WILL FOREVER QUIET ITS THIRST FOR BLOOD."

"Ha-a-a-a, George, look, look at that stupid inscription. I, Doctor Chandu, have found the lost notebook of that great master of life and death, that supreme juggler of natural existence, Professor Bartok. He is dead but his notes will tell me how to bring life to the . . . HUMAN VAMPIRE!"

"What I like, Doctor, is how I choked the keeper of the vault where this coffin was. His eyes bulged so when I dug my fingers into his th. . . ."

"Shut up, you idiot! We can't stand here! The moon will rise soon and the stake must be removed!"

"Yes, master!"

"But, first, is IT ready?"

"If the emergency arises, it will be ready!"

Then, the horrible work began. Slowly, the top of the coffin was lifted. And, as the fresh air seeped into the box, a strange, heavy air was pushed out. Finally, the coffin was open!

"Oh, master!"

"Yes, George, he doesn't look very pretty, does he? How long it has been since his lips have tasted the sweetness of human blood!"

The two men continued to look down on the monster. What did it look like? Imagine a man whose body is thin and long. Imagine a man whose arms, covered by a black cloak, look like the wings of a bat. Imagine a man whose lips are thin and blue . . . lips which hide teeth as sharp as razors.

"All right, George, help me take out the body and place it on this slab. The moonlight must fall directly on the body!"

After the vampire was placed on the specially constructed slab, the doctor retreated to a corner and began to chant strangely. Again and again he would look at the notebook. Then, he removed a hypodermic needle from his bag. In it was a serum prepared in his laboratory from notes in Bartok's book. All was ready now.

"Master, the moon."

The full, silvery moon was rising. The vault began to grow light . . . to shimmer in the strange glow. Doctor Chandu approached the human vampire. He uttered some words. Then, he plunged the needle into the arm of the vampire.

George watched in dumb horror as Chandu began to pull the stake out of the vampire's heart. Slowly . . . slowly, the wooden stake was eased out.

"HA-HAH-HA . . . So. I have life again. But I need blood . . . blood . . . blood!"

The vampire was alive. Quickly, it jumped from the coffin, grabbed George, who was standing nearby, and began to tear at his throat.

"Master . . . help . . . arrrgh. . . ."

"Drink deeply, my pretty. As my slave, you will have much work to do!"

"I, your slave? Ha-ha-ahaaaa. Do you think I would let a human tell me what to do, now that I have been released from death?"

"Stay back! I am your master! I gave you life! STAY BACK!"

The vampire began to come forward. In mad desperation, Doctor Chandu ran to an object he had prepared before.

"It is good I took this precaution. I thought you might be hard to handle. I. . . ."

The vampire was hypnotizing Chandu. In seconds, Chandu was like stone. However, in that state, the doctor could not stand. He pitched forward, slamming heavily into his machine.

"AAAARRRGH!!!"

Back staggered the human vampire, a huge stake driven completely through its chest! The machine was a large sling, capable of shooting wooden stakes!

The monster slumped to the ground, dead! Then, Doctor Chandu dizzily rose to his feet, still in the hypnotic trance. By chance, he rubbed against the coffin and wiped the rust off the *rest* of the inscription.

". . . AND HE WHO IS HYPNOTIZED BY THE VAMPIRE AND IS NOT BROUGHT BACK TO NORMAL BEFORE THE NEXT FULL MOON BY THE VAMPIRE WILL CHANGE INTO A VAMPIRE HIMSELF."

THE THING! THAT GREW!

FROM THE SPINE-CHILLING SLEEP OF A *LIVING DEATH*, FROM THE *UNBELIEVABLE HORROR* OF A *MILLION YEARS AGO*, FROM A *FORGOTTEN ICE-CAVE* DEEP IN THE *TOMB OF THE EARTH* COMES THE *MONSTROUS* TERROR OF...

GREAT SCOTT! A PERFECTLY PRESERVED *BABY DINOSAUR*... FROZEN INTO THE ICE A MILLION YEARS AGO! I MUST TAKE IT BACK TO MY LABORATORY... MAYBE I CAN *BRING IT TO LIFE*...!!

DR. MARVELLE, THE WORLD'S MOST BRILLIANT EXPLORER AND SCIENTIST, TOOK THE DINOSAUR BACK TO HIS *SECLUDED LABORATORY* IN VERMONT. IN SECRECY, HE TINKERED WITH THE STAGGERING SECRETS OF LIFE...

IF ONLY I AM DOING THE *RIGHT THING*... IN THE INTEREST OF SCIENCE! I THINK...THIS EXPERIMENT WILL BRING THE *BEAST* BACK TO LIFE...!

I'VE FOUND IT! THIS IS IT...*THE SECRET OF LIFE*!!

NOW TO LET IT *SLEEP* IN THE LIQUID I HAVE JUST DISCOVERED!

BUT WHEN DR. MARVELLE CAME INTO THE LAB THE NEXT MORNING, HE FELT THE *HAND OF HORROR* TOUCH HIS TINGLING SPINE...

IT'S— IT'S GONE! THAT WINDOW...*SOMETHING* HAS GONE THROUGH THAT *WINDOW!*

GASP!...THE MONSTER HAS *GROWN!* WHAT IF IT DOESN'T STOP GROWING..! WHA-! WHAT WAS THAT NOISE FROM THE MOORS--?!

GRAAAOOWWWWRR!!

GOOD LORD! THERE—THERE IT IS! I MUST FIND SOME WAY TO KILL IT BEFORE IT *GROWS* ANY MORE!!

Spurred BY *TERROR*, DR. MARVELLE WORKED ALL DAY TO FIND A FORMULA THAT WOULD *KILL* THE DINOSAUR BUT, THAT NIGHT...

IT'S...NO USE... I CAN'T KILL THE MONSTER I'VE CREATED! WHAT'S *THAT* AGAINST THE SKY...NO! OH, *NO! IT CAN'T BE!...!*

IT'S—COMING BACK HERE...HELLO! HELLO! OPERATOR! GIVE ME THE POLICE... *EMERGENCY...* I'VE GOT TO RUN! IT'S COMING *NEARER!*

The WEIGHT OF THE HUGE ANIMAL KNOCKED THE EARTH OUT OF ITS ORBIT AND SENT IT WHIRLING TOWARD THE SUN...AND DESTRUCTION.!!

WE'RE - FLYING - *INTO THE SUN!* WE'LL ALL BE DESTROYED! I NEVER SHOULD HAVE TAMPERED WITH THE *PROBLEMS OF LIFE*...AND DEATH!!

BARRROOooOOOOM.!

HELP! HELP!...HUH? WHEWWW.!! IT WAS JUST A...*DREAM!* BUT I'M GOING RIGHT DOWN TO THE LAB AND *DESTROY* THE DINOSAUR....*JUST IN CASE!!*

Dizzy WITH *HORROR,* MARVELLE FOUND THE LAB EXACTLY THE WAY IT WAS....*IN THE NIGHTMARE!!*

IT...CAN'T... BE...

A *HUGE FOOTPRINT!* NOW IT'S REAL!!!

GRROOOWWR!

THE END

TCHES
ALES
WE DARE YOU
TO READ THESE EERIE TALES
FROM OUT OF THIS WORLD!
WITCHES
TALES
MAGAZINE
THRILLING
YARNS OF
SUSPENSE
HE WAS A GUINEA PIG FOR THE...
DEMON FLIES!

WITCHES TALES, DECEMBER, 1954, VOL. 1, NO. 28, IS PUBLISHED BI-MONTHLY by WITCHES TALES, INC., 1860 Broadway, New York 23, N. Y. Entered as second class matter at the Post Office at New York, N. Y., under the Act of March, 3, 1879. Single copies, 10c. Subscription rates, 10 issues for $1.00 in the U. S. and possessions, elsewhere $1.50. All names in this periodical are entirely fictitious and no identification with actual persons is intended. Contents copyrighted, 1954, by Witches Tales, inc., New York, City. Printed in the U.S.A. Title registered in U. S. Patent Office.

GOOD EVENING!

Come in, my friends, come in! This biting, raw January wind will do you ill if you stand out there. Let the warmth of my fire caress your bones and stop their trembling. Haaaa... hee!

Eh? You say the flames in the pit curl high! Heh, heh! Of course! From their depths, I have forged another spine-tingling issue of WITCHES TALES!

Hear me now... come close. I have gathered in this issue a collection of tales never before seen by HUMAN eyes — tales calculated to freeze your blood and tear at your conscience.

TOYS OF TERROR is the first of them. Toys, ordinary toys, become the instruments of horror that terrify a whole city. Their mechanical minds obey the commands of a witch and their hands seek a pair of eyes... perhaps yours!

In THE WITCH WHO WORE WHITE, the true nature of people is explained as two of them call upon the powers of evil for help. The price they pay will shock your sanity!

What terror drones closer and closer to the unsuspecting victims? Why does the mad scientist send his stinging horde out on their journey of death? Read the DEMON FLIES!

Last, but certainly not least, my dear friends, feel the hair on the neck crawl as you read the MAN WHO HAD NO BODY! See a living dead man prowl the streets seeking revenge... seeking a revenge from the tomb!

Ahhhh... I must leave you for a while. But do not despair. The fire will burn until I return and from its light you can read this... the latest diary of weird, supernatural stories...

A *DOLL* WITH NO *EYES*!!

COME WITH ME, MY *PRETTIES*! I CAN SERVE YOU BETTER THAN THE MISTRESS WHO TOSSED YOU AWAY!!

WITHIN THE *CRUMBLING* WALLS OF HER ROOM; THE *LOATHESOME* DEMON UTTERS TERRIBLE WORDS WHICH SET IN MOTION THE *UNSPEAKABLE* FORCES THAT LURK IN THE DARKEST RECESSES OF THE EARTH!...

HEAR ME, POWERS OF DARKNESS AND EVIL!! GRANT THE GIFT OF *LIFE* TO THESE TOYS SO THAT THEY MAY SERVE ME!

SEE!!...SEE HOW THEY BEGIN TO *GROW*...AND *GROW*!!

THEY *LIVE*... AND *BREATHE*...!! GROWR·R·R!!

SUDDENLY A VOICE OTHER THAN THE WITCH'S BREAKS UPON THE SCENE OF HORROR...A VOICE *THICK* WITH THE DEADLY POISON OF *MALICE*... AND *CUNNING*...

I AM THE ONLY ONE WHO CAN *SPEAK*, MIDNIGHT HAG!! MY NAME IS *DIABLO*!... WHAT IS IT YOU WISH. US TO DO?

ONLY AT *NIGHT* WILL YOU HAVE THE LIFE YOU HAVE NOW --- BY DAY YOU WILL BE *POWERLESS*, MERE *TOYS* TO BE SCUFFED AND BEATEN!! BUT THIS IS YOUR *FIRST* TASK, MY FRIENDS...

...TO FIND SUITABLE *EYES* FOR THIS PRETTY YOUNG THING WHOM I SHALL CALL *MADELEINE*. THESE EYES MIGHT BE TAKEN FROM ANYONE -- *ANYONE AT ALL!!*

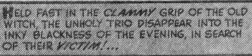

HELD FAST IN THE *CLAMMY* GRIP OF THE OLD WITCH, THE UNHOLY TRIO DISAPPEAR INTO THE INKY BLACKNESS OF THE EVENING, IN SEARCH OF THEIR *VICTIM!*...

GO, MY CREATURES OF DEATH! THE NIGHT IS STILL YOUNG --- AND HUMAN BLOOD IS *FRESH* AND *WARM!!*

LATER... I WONDER WHAT'S KEEPING THE BUS---

LINOLEUM

CARPETS

BUS STOP

WHAT--NO!! NO!! **HELP!!**

YAAH-H-H-H!! **ROWR-R!! GROWRR-R-R!!**

IT'S LIKE SOME *INHUMAN BEAST* WAS TRYING TO RIP HIM TO *PIECES!* UGG-H-H!!

BUT WHY DID HE TEAR OUT HIS *EYES??!*

AND STILL THE "TOYS" STALK THE STREETS OF THE CITY, *UNSATISFIED* IN THEIR *GHASTLY* SEARCH, FORCED BY THE WILL OF THE OLD WITCH TO LUNGE *WILDLY* AT ALL THOSE WHO CROSS THEIR PATH!...

I'LL SEE IF I CAN GET A CLEARER PICTURE---

MAKE IT A LITTLE LOUDER, TOO, I THINK---

AH-H-H!!

WHO ARE YOU? *WHAT* ARE YOU???

STOP THEIR MOUTHS!! *KILL* THEM-- AND TAKE THEIR *EYES!!* THE LAST PAIR DIDN'T DO!

ARRGHH-H-H-H!!

AS LIGHT BEGINS TO PIERCE THE DARKNESS, THE THREE CREATURES ANXIOUSLY SEEK THEIR REFUGE WITH THE WITCH, AFRAID THAT *LIFE* WILL BE TAKEN FROM THEM WITH THE SUN!...

BACK! BACK!! DAYLIGHT IS COMING!!

WELL, MY FRIENDS!! STILL NO SATISFACTION, NO PRETTY *PAIR* OF *EYES* FOR SWEET MADELEINE!! HAVE NO FEAR--- YOU SHALL *CONTINUE!!!*

ALONE IN HER ROOM, THE *DECAYING* WITCH AWAITS THE RETURN OF HER CREATURES, HER *REPULSIVE* FACE LIT BY AN UGLY SMILE OF SATISFACTION...

THEY WILL RETURN SOON! IT IS GETTING *LIGHT!*

AH, I KNEW YOU WOULD COME BACK!! I AM DELIGHTED TO SEE YOU!!

OUR SEARCH FOR A PAIR OF EYES HAS BEEN *FUTILE* UNTIL NOW, FIEND OF DARKNESS!! BUT WE MUST TEST *ONE MORE PAIR --- ONLY ONE --*!!

...AND THEY ARE *YOURS!!!*

KILL ME, WILL YOU? FOOLS! YOU HAVE THE *BRAINS OF TOYS!!* I UTTER THIS CURSE UPON YOU: YOU WILL BE *HORRIBLY DESTROYED* BECAUSE YOU ARE *NOTHING* WITHOUT ME!

RAWRR-R!

SCREECHING HER LAST *HIDEOUS* CURSE, THE OLD WITCH FEELS THE *POWERFUL* ARMS OF THE APE SHE CREATED *PRESS* AGAINST HER THROAT... *TIGHTER....TIGHTER...*

AAARRGGH-H!

RUN!! RUN WITH ME!! WE MUST FIND SOME PLACE TO *HIDE* BEFORE IT IS *LIGHT!!*

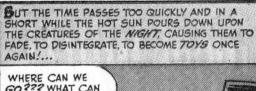

BUT THE TIME PASSES TOO QUICKLY AND IN A SHORT WHILE THE HOT SUN POURS DOWN UPON THE CREATURES OF THE *NIGHT*, CAUSING THEM TO FADE, TO DISINTEGRATE, TO BECOME *TOYS* ONCE AGAIN!...

WHERE CAN WE GO??? WHAT CAN WE DO-O-O-O...?

TOYS!! OLD, BATTERED TOYS! WHAT GOOD ARE THEY TO ANYBODY? *I* CAN'T EVEN USE THEM!!

JUNK BOUGHT & SOLD RAGS, SCRAP OLD CLOTH

THIS SHOULD TAKE CARE OF THEM, I GUESS! I COULDN'T GET A PLUG NICKEL FOR THEM --- EVEN FROM A *KID!*

DEPARTMENT OF SANITATION

SAY, BUD, DO YOU HEAR ANY *STRANGE NOISES* COMING FROM THE INCINERATOR?

I DON'T THINK SO --- MUST BE THE MECHANISM *GRINDING* UP THE GARBAGE!!

YAAH-H-H!! AAH-H-H-H!!

AIEEE-EE! ARGGH-H-H!

GRAWRRR!! AWRR-RR!!

AS THE INCINERATOR *CRUSHES* EVERYTHING THAT FALLS INTO ITS IRON JAWS, A FEW LOW SCREAMS OF ANGUISH CAN BE HEARD --- AND THEN THERE IS ONLY A *TERRIBLE --* AND *COMPLETE --* SILENCE!...

COULD'VE SWORN I HEARD *HUMAN SCREAMS* COMING FROM THERE!

THE END.

THE WITCH WHO WORE WHITE

STRANGE THINGS HAPPEN IN THE NIGHT, AND HOW TERRIBLE WAS THE CONTRAST WHEN THE MURKY BLACKNESS OF THE NIGHT BECAME THE BACKGROUND FOR...

WH--WHAT ARE YOU GOING TO *DO* TO ME?

YOU MUST PAY THE *PRICE* I SET!! THERE IS NO ESCAPE!!

OH, NO! WHAT *UNNATURAL CREATURE* IS LOOSE IN THIS HOUSE??

IN THE HOME OF FABULOUSLY WEALTHY ARTHUR AND ABIGAIL SANDERS, A NEWCOMER APPEARS, A YOUNG GIRL WHOSE WHITE NURSE'S UNIFORM IS MATCHED BY THE *STRANGE* WHITENESS OF HER FACE...

ARTHUR, DEAR, THIS IS MISS JESSUP, YOUR NEW *NURSE!* I'M SURE SHE'LL PLEASE YOU!

BAH.!! SHE'S PROBABLY AS STUPID AND INCOMPETENT AS THE OTHERS!

I HOPE YOU WILL FIND ME SATISFACTORY!

HELLO, PAUL! I'D LIKE YOU TO MEET MISS JESSUP, OUR NEW NURSE. PAUL'S MY NEPHEW--- HE'S BEEN LIVING WITH US A WHILE!

HOW DO YOU DO, MISS JESSUP?

THE *ODDLY QUIET* MANNER, THE *GHOST-LIKE* FACE OF THE NURSE STIRS A CURIOSITY IN THE NEPHEW WHICH SETS HIM TO WONDERING...

SHE SEEMS *DIFFERENT* SOMEHOW FROM THE OTHERS---AS IF SHE DIDN'T *BELONG* HERE! I FEEL AS IF SHE'S AWARE OF MY INTEREST IN THE *SANDERS FORTUNE!!*

*A*ND AS THE DAYS PASS, PAUL IS NOT THE ONLY MEMBER OF THE HOUSE-HOLD TO BE PLAGUED WITH CURIOSITY

THERE SHE IS AGAIN! SHE ONLY MOVES ABOUT AT NIGHT-- WITH THAT *CANDLE!* SHE TAKES GOOD CARE OF ARTHUR BUT SHE *FRIGHTENS* ME! I WONDER...

I'LL OPEN THE DOOR VERY *QUIETLY*--AND LOOK IN QUICKLY! I MUST FIND OUT---

OH, SACRED RULER OF THE *CULT OF WITCHES,* HEAR THESE WORDS OF YOUR DISCIPLE!! MAY *EVIL* AND *HORROR* DESCEND UPON HUMANITY UNTIL THEY WRITHE IN *ANGUISH* AND *DESPAIR---!!*

OH-H-H-H-H

WHAT *MONSTER* OF *EVIL* ARE YOU? WHAT ARE YOU DOING IN MY HOUSE?

WELL!! YOU HAVE DISCOVERED MY *SECRET!!* THERE IS NO LONGER ANY NEED TO PRETEND WITH *YOU!*--'I AM A *WITCH,* DEDICATED TO THE DESTRUCTION OF MAN---

*T*HE *SHOCKING* REVELATION BRINGS NO TERROR TO THE OLD WOMAN'S FACE, NO FEAR, NO LOATHING--- BUT ONLY A SUDDEN *GRIMNESS* AND *DETERMINATION...*

IF YOU ARE WHAT YOU SAY, THEN YOU CAN *HELP* ME! YOU CAN HELP ME TO *DESTROY* MY *HUSBAND!!* I CAN'T TOLERATE HIS ENDLESS WHINING ANY LONGER!!

I SEE THAT *HUMAN EVIL* EXISTS EVERYWHERE... BUT I *ACCEPT* YOUR KIND OFFER! I HAVE TWO DEMANDS, HOWEVER: YOU MUST LET *ME* DESTROY YOUR HUSBAND IN *MY OWN WAY*--- AND YOU MUST PAY THE PRICE FOR MY *SERVICES* WHEN I DEMAND IT!!

VERY WELL! I AGREE!!

*B*UT BARGAINS IN *EVIL* ARE EASILY MADE ...AND A SHORT WHILE LATER, ANOTHER UNHOLY CONTRACT IS FORMED WITH THE *DEMON-NURSE*...

I CAN SEE IN YOUR EYES THAT YOU ARE LIKE *ME*-- DETERMINED TO GET WHAT YOU CAN BY FAIR MEANS AND *FOUL*...MY AUNT AND UNCLE ARE VERY *OLD* AND VERY *RICH.!!* NEED I SAY MORE?

NO, PAUL-- YOU *NEEDN'T!*

WHAT IS YOUR PRICE FOR HELPING MY AUNT AND UNCLE TO MEET A *SUDDEN* END?

THIS HOUSE-- AND NOTHING *MORE!!* THE MONEY IS FOR YOU TO *KEEP!!*

*L*ATE THAT NIGHT, A *WEIRD* FIGURE APPEARS BEFORE THE OLD MAN'S BED-- AND BEFORE HIS WIDENING EYES CONJURES A *LOATHESOME, ROTTING* CREATURE OUT OF THE DARKNESS!...

MISS JESSUP! N--N--O--O!! IT CAN'T BE!!!

TREBORAT SORFROUNTA TABORAI!!

DIE!! DIE!! DIE!!

YAAAAH!!

*T*HE NEXT MORNING THE OLD MAN'S BODY IS FOUND, A *GHASTLY* MOUND OF FLESH THAT SEEMS TO HAVE BEEN DEVOURED BY SOME *BEAST* OF PREY!...

UGHHH-H-H.!!! HOW COULD THIS HAVE HAPPENED DURING THE *NIGHT*?

I DON'T *KNOW!!* POOR, DEAR ARTHUR!!

AS PAUL WRESTS THE SCALPEL FROM THE NURSE'S HAND, HE TRIPS AND FALLS ACROSS THE BED...

UGH-H-H!!!

AARGH-H-H-H!!

I---I-- KILLED HER!!

ISN'T THAT WHAT YOU WANTED? BUT NOW YOU WILL NEVER ESCAPE FROM THIS HOUSE, MY FRIEND!! YOU WILL ROT HERE WITH YOUR AUNT AND UNCLE!!

A FEW WORDS OF ANCIENT EVIL--AND BLOOD-STAINED DEMONS OF THE NIGHT APPEAR ABOVE THE HEAD OF THE WITCH-NURSE---EAGER FOR HUMAN PREY!

LABRUNTA! SAIGORA! TAKE HIM!! HE IS YOURS!!

YAAAAAH-H

LEAVE ME ALONE!! NO!! DON'T!! D---

YAAGGH-H!

AND NOW THIS HOUSE IS MINE--MINE TO DESTROY--AS I CAUSE EVIL TO DESTROY THE HEARTS AND MINDS OF MEN!!

IN ANOTHER HOME, A PALE YOUNG NURSE APPEARS IN THE DOORWAY, AN ANGEL OF MERCY ANSWERING A CALL TO DUTY ...BUT WHAT IS THE STRANGE DREAD THAT SUDDENLY STIFLES THE NIGHT AIR??...

HOW DO YOU DO? YOU MUST BE...

MISS JESSUP! AT YOUR SERVICE...!!

THE END

SUICIDE!

"What's the matter, my dear?"

"Nothing, Margaret.... Nothing at all."

"But Dr. Wilson just left your chamber."

"A routine check-up. Yes, Margaret, that's all it was...a routine check-up."

Mrs. Van Dyke left the room. She didn't fully believe her husband, but she saw that he was in no mood for questions.

Left alone, Cecil Van Dyke began to wonder. He searched the corners of his sumptuously decorated room. The light bothered him. He turned it off. So much easier to think this way, he thought.

"I've got to face it," Van Dyke said to himself. "All Dr. Wilson gives me is six months to live. Probably less."

He paced back and forth across his room.

"Margaret must never know...but why does it have to happen to ME? I'm the most important man in the industry! I've worked and worked for years and now that I'm on top of the world, I discover I'm about to die."

Van Dyke's steps became slower.

"He doesn't even know what kind of disease this is. Never saw it before, he said. But he does know that I'm slowly melting away inside. I'm disintegrating! I'm wasting away."

Van Dyke stopped and dropped onto the couch.

"I knew I was sick, but I could never have expected this! Those X-Rays told the evil tale. Those terrible X-Rays! Oh, if I could mould this world, I'd never allow X-Rays! Let me die, but why must I know every step of disintegration!"

He broke into a sweat. His face became ghost-like!

"I know what I must do! I'VE GOT TO KILL MYSELF! I mustn't make Margaret miserable. And I couldn't stand seeing myself melt away slowly...like a candle!"

He rushed to lock the door. Then he went to his desk. He slowly opened the drawer and took out his pistol. "Well, this gun will stop a murder," he thought.

Then there was a noise and a knocking at the door.

"Cecil, open the door!"

No one was going to stop him! The doctor had probably told her. No, he wasn't going to make any one miserable, he wasn't going to stretch this out!

"Cecil, open the door!!!"

"Good-bye, my dear!"

BANG!

"Darling, what was that explosion? I want to tell you that the doctor had the wrong X-Rays!"

THE MASK OF DEATH!

"They laugh! They laugh and laugh at me!"

"Bill, stop it! How can you complain? You're one of the greatest night club comedians of our time! Sure, people laugh at you, that's what you're paid for. And your face is perfect for..."

"Hah! That's it, even you, you're laughing at me. See—HAH! HAH! HAH! That's what you want to do. Look, my whole face is scarred! Is that funny??"

"Yes, Bill, it is. I don't know why, but you do look silly."

"Yes, hah hah! You, my wife, even you can't stop laughing at me. Ouch! This damn pin!"

"Hah, hah. Bill. You look so funny!"

"I cut myself and you laugh! When I get sick, you laugh! If I died, you'd still laugh! In fact, you'd roar. In fact, you only married me for my money. Now, I'm just one big laugh from morning till night! HAH! HAH! HAH!"

"Bill, stop it! Yes, it's true. I did marry you for your money. And now I'm tired of your stupid face, your fat and comical body, your...STOP IT! KEEP AWAY FROM ME!"

"HAH! HAH! No, my beautiful doll! You've had your last laugh! Hah! That's pretty good... In a few moments you're going to speak your LAST WORDS!"

"Bill, put down that knife! I didn't mean it!"

"Yes, I'll put it down—right down your throat! I've had enough—enough, you hear!"

He rushed to her and swung his knife—once, twice, three times...

"AHHHHHHH!"

Then the house was quiet. In it, a beautiful woman lay dead, and a man, ghost-white and silent, bent motionless over her.

The man picked himself up. He took the knife —and raised it high above him...

"HAH! HAH! HAH! AGHHHH!"

It wasn't until the next morning that people came to this house, this home far in the suburbs. There they discovered a once beautiful woman. No words could express their horror.

In the other corner, they saw Bill West, the great comic. Even in death there was that silly expression all over him ... They tried to stop themselves, but they just had to laugh!

THE MAN WHO HAD NO BODY

SCREAMING THRU THE BLACK NIGHT, TWO TRAINS RACE TOWARD EACH OTHER IN AN UNKNOWN *APPOINTMENT WITH DEATH!!* THE SCREAMS OF THE VICTIMS MIX WITH A DISTANT *EVIL WAIL* AND OUT OF THE FIRE AND BLOOD OF THIS *MIDNIGHT* CATASTROPHE WALKS...

SCREAM AND *WAIL*, YOU POWERLESS MORTALS! HEE-HEE! IT'S MUSIC TO MY EARS. *NONE* OF YOU CAN ESCAPE THE *HANDS OF FATE!!* HEE-HEEEEEE!

HELP!

HELP!

OHOOOOo...

EEEEEE!!

CRASH, BA-LOOOM!

WH...WHERE AM I?? OH- NOW I REMEMBER... WAITING TO GET OFF...THEN A CRASH...AN EXPLOSION!! OHOOO- MY HEAD...

TONY LAWSON WAS JUST ANOTHER PASSENGER ON THE ILL-FATED TRAIN, ANXIOUS TO RETURN TO HIS WIFE. HE HAD YET TO LEARN THAT THE CRASH HAD JOLTED HIM INTO A *NEW, WEIRD* WORLD...

MY HEAD FEELS AS IF SOMEBODY WERE BOILING MY BRAINS!! PEOPLE HURT ...MUST TRY TO HELP...

HELLLLPP!! THE FIRE !! ARGHHH!

MORE *WATER!!* PEOPLE ARE *TRAPPED* IN THERE!!

(SOB-SOB... SOB-SOB)

TAKE IT EASY BABY... DON'T OVERDO IT!!

A GRAVEYARD IS A *BIG* PLACE... THERE IS ROOM FOR *MANY MORE* IN THE *FAMILY CRYPT!*

...AND MAY TONY LAWSON, WHO MET DEATH SO EARLY IN LIFE AS THE RESULT OF AN UNFORTUNATE ACCIDENT, FIND *EVERLASTING* PEACE...

I...I FEEL SO *COLD*, JOHN... I FEEL AS IF I WERE BEING *WATCHED*—AS IF SOMEBODY ...SOMETHING... WERE *LAUGHING* AT ME!!

C'MON—LET'S GET OUT OF HERE! IN A FEW DAYS THEY'LL *CEMENT* THAT CASKET AWAY, AND *THAT* WILL BE THE *END* OF IT!!

POOR TONY... I'LL NEVER BE ABLE TO GO ON WITHOUT HIM!

THERE, THERE, LUCY ...YOU MUST BEAR UP!

TIME WILL HEAL YOUR WOUND...

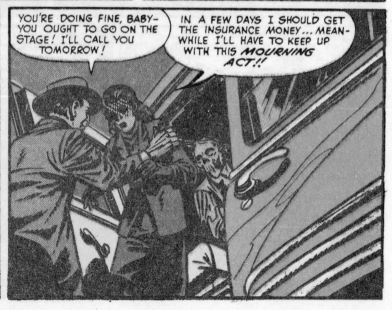

YOU'RE DOING FINE, BABY—YOU OUGHT TO GO ON THE STAGE! I'LL CALL YOU TOMORROW!

IN A FEW DAYS I SHOULD GET THE INSURANCE MONEY... MEAN-WHILE I'LL HAVE TO KEEP UP WITH THIS *MOURNING ACT!!*

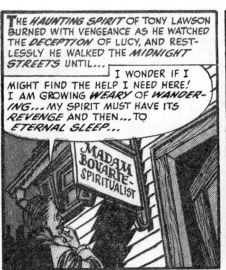

THE *HAUNTING SPIRIT* OF TONY LAWSON BURNED WITH VENGEANCE AS HE WATCHED THE *DECEPTION* OF LUCY, AND RESTLESSLY HE WALKED THE *MIDNIGHT STREETS* UNTIL...

I WONDER IF I MIGHT FIND THE HELP I NEED HERE! I AM GROWING *WEARY* OF *WANDERING*...MY SPIRIT MUST HAVE ITS *REVENGE* AND THEN...TO *ETERNAL SLEEP*...

MADAM BOVARIE- SPIRITUALIST

MIDNIGHT WANDERERS...,HEAR MY CALL! I WOULD SEND MY VOICE BEYOND THE *UNKNOWN* TO TALK WITH THE *RESTLESS ONES*, THE *SPIRITS* WHO SEEK *POWER*... HEAR ME, *UNSEEN ONES*, OH, HEAR!!

I HAVE HEARD....AND I HAVE COME TO ASK YOU WHO *SPEAK WITH THE DEAD* FOR *HELP!!*

YES...I WILL HELP YOU... FOR A *FEE!!* FOR EVEN THE *DEAD* MUST PAY THE *BLACK SORCERERS!!*

YOU WILL BE WELL PAID... NOW, FIRST YOU MUST WRITE A LETTER FOR ME...

AND SO... IN THE *DEAD OF NIGHT* THE BARGAIN IS MADE, AND A FEW DAYS LATER...

I KNOW YOU EXPECTED THE MONEY, BUT WE JUST RECEIVED THIS LETTER, SIGNED BY YOUR *HUSBAND*, TONY LAWSON!!

BUT...BUT THAT'S *IMPOSSIBLE!!* I IDENTIFIED THE BODY MYSELF- AND IT'S LYING IN THE FAMILY *CRYPT!!* THIS IS SOMEBODY'S *CRUEL JOKE!!*

OF COURSE IT IS! UNDOUBTEDLY YOU ARE PERFECTLY RIGHT, BUT WE WILL HAVE TO INVESTIGATE THIS LETTER BEFORE WE CAN TURN THE MONEY OVER!

ALL RIGHT- JUST AS LONG AS IT WON'T TAKE TOO LONG! AS A MATTER OF FACT, I'M GOING TO THE CRYPT TODAY- TO BRING FRESH FLOWERS! I MISS TONY SO...

I'LL BE GLAD WHEN THEY'VE FINALLY CEMENTED THIS CASKET AWAY SO I DON'T HAVE TO KEEP UP THIS *PRETENSE* OF DEVOTION!! WONDER ABOUT THAT LETTER! WHO...OH!!!

LATER THAT NIGHT THE TWO FIGURES, ONE SEEN AND THE OTHER *UNSEEN*, WALK THRU THE *DESERTED GRAVEYARD* TO THE LAWSON CRYPT, AND THERE...

I HAVE ONE MORE REQUEST TO MAKE! I AM WEARY OF BEING A *DISEMBODIED SPIRIT!* PUT ME BACK INSIDE MY *MANGLED BODY...* I HAVE A *PLAN!*

I WILL DO AS YOU ASK—ONLY REMEMBER, ONCE IT IS DONE NO POWER CAN UNDO IT!!

MAR RION BEL EF FANTOV LORREL TON!!

THE NEXT DAY... IT WILL SOON BE OVER! TODAY THE CASKET WILL BE *SEALED AWAY!* SHALL I GO IN WITH YOU?

YES...NO! THIS IS THE LAST TIME... I'LL GO IN ALONE FOR A FEW MINUTES! IT WILL LOOK BETTER!

ALONE, LUCY LAWSON APPROACHES THE CASKET FOR THE LAST TIME, ANXIOUS FOR THE FINAL CEREMONY TO BEGIN, WHEN SUDDENLY...

THAT'S STRANGE THAT THE TOP SHOULD BE OPEN... WELL, SOON I'LL BE FREE OF THIS AWFUL TASK... AND JOHN AND I...

HIS HANDS!...THEY'RE *MOVING!!* TONY... NO.!!!

DON'T, TONY...*PLEASE!!* I'LL DO ANYTHING YOU SAY! I WON'T TOUCH THE MONEY...I'LL GIVE JOHN UP... I'LL...

THE *POINTED EDGE OF DEATH* SLOWLY INCHES TOWARD THE SOFT, PULSATING THROAT OF LUCY LAWSON!! HER EYES STRAIN WITH *TERROR*, HER STRENGTH WANS, AND *THEN*...

AIEEEEGRGHGGAGG!!

GREAT SCOTT—WHAT WAS *THAT??!*

OH, THE POOR THING! SHE'S *KILLED HERSELF!*

GUESS SHE *COULDN'T LIVE* WITHOUT HIM!!

THE END.

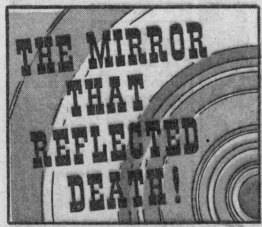

THE MIRROR THAT REFLECTED DEATH!

"I've come to you, old hag, because I have no one left to turn to."

"Ha...heeee...most people who come here say that. What troubles you?"

"For the past month I have been having awful nightmares. I dream I see myself in a mirror not as I really am but as some horrible beast. When I see myself so, I go insane and hurl myself at this mirror shattering the glass into a thousand pieces. I wake up then...my face coated with sweat...my throat choked with a sobbing gasp."

Lamont Wilson looked at the old woman he was talking to. He, the richest man in the city, was forced to come to her, a known practitioner of the black arts, for help. Dr. Runsen, his private psychiatrist, said it was a case of too much work, not enough rest. He said it would be best if Wilson went to a sanitarium for a few months.

"In other words," thought Wilson, "he thinks I'm going crazy."

"I see you are deep in thought," cackled the old witch, her face deeply wrinkled by the candle light.

"Uh-yes. And you probably know what I am thinking about. Look...I will give you any amount of money if you can cure me of those terrible nightmares. I..."

"Wait! Before you speak any further, let me speak."

The light from the two candles in the room began to flicker. Shadows began to close in about the room and the mist of mystery slowly slid over the woman. Her eyes narrowed to slits and the blood began to drain from her cheeks.

"Listen to what I say, mortal. It is what will be. I know that your doctor thinks you are going crazy. He thinks it is overwork...straining of the nerves. I know the real reason!"

"Old hag, tell me quick!"

"Quiet! Never interrupt me! You are having those dreams because you want to *murder* someone!"

Lamont Wilson fell back in his chair. Beads of perspiration began to pop out on his face. His hands crushed the arm rests of the chair.

"M-m-murder! I don't want to murder anyone."

"Ha...heeee...you do, you do. And here's why, whimpering mortal. All your life you have been beating people down...taking what you wanted. First you drove your partner out of business. Then you began to hire the cheapest labor you could...slave labor. You kept on smashing to the top regardless of the consequences. Now, you are at the top. You have done everything. You have done everything, that is, except...MURDER! And though you are really too weak to do it, you cannot sleep without seeing yourself the true monster you are lusting for human blood. You are one of us, Lamont Wilson. And you will MURDER...haaa...heeeee..."

As the last of the witch's words pierced his brain, Wilson tore himself up from the chair and plunged out of the house into the street. Panic ripped his mind to shreds. Why should her words affect him so. Why? Why? Could she be right?

Wilson kept on running...running. Soon, his tired feet brought him to a cheap carnival. In a daze of fear, he rushed up to a booth and bought a ticket. Unseeing, he staggered inside and discovered...

"NO! I'm in the HALL OF MIRRORS!"

He tried to get out but some strange force seemed to pull him to a certain mirror. When he saw the image on it, he gasped...

"That's the beast I've been seeing in my dreams. ARRRRGGGHHHH..."

Lamont Wilson had hurled himself against the mirror.

Later, two policemen talked with the owner of the exhibit.

"That's all I know, officers. I heard this scream, rushed in and found this crazy guy on the floor dead. It looks like he threw himself at the mirror and got knifed by the broken glass."

"You know," said one of the cops, "this guy really was a murderer. He murdered...himself!"

AND AS THE SCIENTIST REGARDS THE ODD *REVERSAL* OF *NATURE*, A *DREADFUL* PLAN BEGINS TO TAKE SHAPE IN HIS *CORRUPT* MIND...

I MAY HAVE DISCOVERED A SPECIES OF FLY MORE *POWERFUL* THAN ANY YET KNOWN, POWERFUL ENOUGH TO BECOME A ...*WEAPON!!* IF IT CAN KILL A SPIDER...

SEVERAL WEEKS LATER...

AT LAST.!! NOW THERE ARE *THOUSANDS* OF LARGE, HUNGRY FLIES BEGGING TO BE *FED!!*

I WAS *RIGHT!!* THESE FLIES ARE LIKE *DEMONS*, ANXIOUS TO CONSUME WHATEVER FALLS IN THEIR *GREEDY* PATH!! NOW I AM READY TO TRY MY GREAT *EXPERIMENT..!*

YOU WANTED ME, DR. GILBERT?

YES, HARDING, WON'T YOU COME IN? AND *CLOSE THE DOOR*, PLEASE!

DOCTOR, YOU WILL BE THE HUMAN GUINEA PIG TO SHOW THAT I HAVE CREATED MONSTERS WHOSE INSTINCTS I CONTROL!

NO!! NO!!

LIKE A *REPULSIVE* ARMY OF *PARASITES*, THE FLIES COVER THEIR VICTIM, TEARING AT HIS FLESH UNTIL HE IS LEFT A *FESTERING* AND *APPALLING* SKELETON!!...

AAARGHH-H-H!!

BZZZ!! BUZZ-Z-Z!

WELL DONE!! NOW I NO LONGER FEAR THAT THEY WILL TURN ON ME!! THEY HAVE SERVED THEIR PURPOSE AND I AM WELL *RID* OF THEM!!

BUT YOU MUST RETURN TO YOUR BOTTLE, MY FRIEND! UNTIL I CAN USE YOU *AGAIN*!!

SUDDENLY, WITHOUT WARNING, THE GIANT SPIDER BEGINS TO WEAVE A *SECOND* WEB, *LARGER* AND *DEADLIER* THAN THE FIRST... ABOUT THE BODY OF THE SCIENTIST.

WH--WHAT ARE YOU *DOING* TO ME?? *STOP!!!* I *COMMAND* YOU!! S---

AND AS THE WEB COVERS THE SCIENTISTS BODY LIKE A *SHROUD*, HE FALLS BACK AGAINST A TABLE, UPSETTING THE BUNSEN BURNER HE HAD LIGHTED FOR AN EXPERIMENT!...

AAAGGH-H-H!!! RAWRRRGGH-H-H!!

CRASH!

AAIIIEEEEE-E-E

AS THE LABORATORY IS DEVOURED BY FLAME, TWO CURIOUS SPECTATORS PERCH OUTSIDE THE WINDOW, WATCHING THE *AGONIZED* DEATH OF THE SCIENTIST-AND THE MONSTER-SPIDER HE HAD CREATED!...

THE END

START YOUR FUTURE TODAY!

Get the facts on NATIONAL SCHOOLS' famous Shop-Method Home Training!

RADIO-TELEVISION
& ELECTRONICS

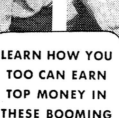

LEARN HOW YOU TOO CAN EARN TOP MONEY IN THESE BOOMING INDUSTRIES!

AUTO-MECHANICS
& DIESEL

A BRIGHT FUTURE awaits you in booming Radio-TV industry. More than 100 million radio sets, 20 million TV sets, now in use! Backed by National Schools' famous Shop-Method Training from America's Radio-TV Capital you can command good wages in the opportunity-career of your choice — engineer, service-repair, inspector, designer — in radar, electronics — or your own profitable business! Make that bright future come true... start now!

WE SEND YOU COMPLETE PARTS, INCLUDING HIGH-MU TUBES!

Yours to keep. You learn by doing, actually build generators, R-F oscillators, and this big Super-Het receiver!

WE SEND YOU THIS STANDARD PROFESSIONAL MULTITESTER! Locates trouble, adjusts delicate circuits—a valuable profit-earner for you when you become a qualified Radio-TV technician!

LET NATIONAL SCHOOLS of Los Angeles, California, a Resident Technical Trade School for nearly half a century, train you at home for a high-paying future in these big-future industries.

Earn While You Learn!

Make extra money repairing friends' and neighbors' cars, trucks, radios, TV sets, appliances. Every step fully explained and illustrated in National Schools' famous "Shop-Tested" lessons. Latest equipment and techniques covered. You master all phases—start part-time earnings after a few weeks'

YOU RECEIVE FRIENDLY GUIDANCE, both as a student and graduate. Our special Welfare Department is always at your service, to help you with technical and personal problems. You receive full benefit of our wide industry contacts and experience.

DRAFT AGE? National Schools training helps you get the service branch, and higher pay grade you want

APPROVED FOR G. I. TRAINING

EXPANDING AUTO-DIESEL INDUSTRY needs more and more trained men! 55 million vehicles now operating, 6 million more this year—plus 150,000 new Diesel units! Garages, car dealers, transit lines, defense plants, manufacturers, are desperate for the kind of *trained specialists* produced by National Schools' "Shop-Method Home Training." Start *now* on the road to lifetime security. Mail the coupon today!

WE SEND YOU THE TOOLS OF YOUR TRADE! This fully-equipped, all-metal Tool Kit is yours to keep. We also send you a complete set of precision drawing instruments, and Slide Rule These professional tools help you learn, then *earn!*

NATIONAL SCHOOLS DEPT. 2F-94
Technical Trade Training Since 1905

LOS ANGELES 37, CALIFORNIA
In Canada: 811 West Hastings Street
Vancouver, B. C.
Both Home Study and Resident Courses Offered

FREE! RADIO-TV BOOK & LESSON!

FREE! AUTO-DIESEL BOOK & LESSON!

MAIL COUPON NOW START YOUR HIGH-PAYING FUTURE TODAY!

GET FACTS FASTEST!
MAIL TO OFFICE NEAREST YOU!

(mail in envelope or paste on postal card)
NATIONAL SCHOOLS, Dept. 2F-94

4000 S. Figueroa Street   or   **323 West Polk Street**
Los Angeles 37, Calif.   **Chicago 7, Ill.**

Please rush *Free Book & Sample Lesson* checked below. No obligation, no salesman will call.

☐ *"My Future in Radio-Television & Electronics"*
☐ *"My Future in Automotive-Diesel & Allied Mechanics"*

NAME_____ BIRTHDAY_____19___

ADDRESS_____

CITY_____ZONE_____STATE_____

☐ Check if interested **ONLY** in Resident School Training at Los Angeles.
VETERANS Give Date of Discharge_____